OLIVO OLIVA

OLIVO OLIVA

PHILIPPE POLONI

A NOVEL

Translated by David Homel

Published in 1999 by Stoddart Publishing Co. Limited
34 Lesmill Road, Toronto, Canada M3B 2T6

Original French edition published in Quebec in 1997 by Lanctôt Éditeur

Distributed by:
General Distribution Services Ltd.
325 Humber College Blvd., Toronto, Canada M9W 7C3
Tel. (416) 213-1919   Fax (416) 213-1917
Email customer.service@ccmailgw.genpub.com

03   02   01   00   99   1   2   3   4   5

Canadian Cataloguing in Publication Data

Poloni, Philippe, 1958-
[Olivo Oliva. English]
Olivo Oliva

Translation of: Olivo Oliva
ISBN 0-7737-6068-7

I. Homel, David. II. Title. III. Title: Olivo Oliva. English.

PS8581.03604413 1999   C843'.54   C99-931466-1
PQ3919.2.P577804413 1999

Cover Design: Angel Guerra
Text Design: Tannice Goddard

*We acknowledge for their financial support of our publishing program the Canada
Council, the Ontario Arts Council, and the Government of Canada through the
Book Publishing Industry Development Program (BPIDP). This book was made
possible in part through the Canada Council's translation grants program.*

Printed and bound in Canada

For Silvio P.

per sempre . . .

Art is art.
— Johann Wolfgang von Goethe

*N*ight isn't black. Night is blue.
Omnipresent, inaccessible, deceiving blue . . .
Physically, black is the absence of radiation from a body
whose surface, by its molecular structure,
captures all visible waves of the chromatic spectrum.
The horned wings of beetles are black.
The underskirts of Sicily, too . . .

Nocturnal blue is a starved kind of black . . .
High above, a tiny sliver of moon tries to light the earth.
In this colossal task it is accompanied by a myriad of stars
that do not move, and a handful of spinning planets . . .
Night is a muse . . .
Ever since Antiquity, poets have declaimed the
blackness of the night. The blacker it is, the crueler
man is to his neighbor!
Yet night is blue . . .

Lovers caress under the Patriarchal Olive Tree.
They are lit by that same sliver of moon,
those same motionless stars and those planets
without luminosity of their own.
Nature seems to have tempered the bluing of the
countryside with a complex play of breezes and
cumulus archipelagos — shadowy enough to
call you to fulfillment, light enough to see
what you're touching . . .

The Olive is black. The kind of black you find under tectonic
plates or in pelagic depths, though that's not sure . . .
The Olive has a soul . . . It is alive . . . At night,
it contemplates the nuances of blue that tint the
olive grove and mystify its forms . . .
The Olive does not recognize black, because it is
blackness itself.
A blackness so penetrating it stupefies the eye and
casts it into the most delectable excess.

I

The Olive was alive. It had a soul.

On those long, fastidious days, pedunculated on the end of its branch, the black fruit meditated. The Olive was making calculations. It was trying to resolve a mathematical equation: how much time does light take to travel between it and a distant object?

Nearby was a young olive tree. A recently planted scion, unproductive, of an ash-green color typical to its species. Its foliage shimmered whenever the sirocco shook it. When that happened, the leaves, with their silky white undersides, reminded the eye of a school of anchovies in sudden dispersal.

But that wasn't the case now. The still landscape grew thick under a furious sun, and the music of the cicadas, drunk with light, was so strident that the poor traveler, unaccustomed to it, would suffer from vertigo.

The young olive tree had a soul. It was possessed of memory. A kind of heredity. Awkwardly, it paraded the military pride of its ancestors. Poor little tree! It was but a simple domesticated olive producer among the millions of other domesticated Mediterranean copies, all planted in rigorously straight rows. No more petalism! Doric temples a thing of the past! Polytheist ceremonies accompanied by chanting and pungent Levantine incense — all obsolete. Its leaf would no longer serve as a model for those early Christian mosaicists who decorated their catacombs, late at night, illuminated by the oil of its fruit. All that had happened, long ago . . . All that belonged to another time. The scion was a heraldic tree no more, but the object of intensive, rationalized agriculture. And the haughty little olive tree knew nothing of that!

The Olive was thinking. It was calculating.

The young olive tree was green because the chloro-phyll contained in its leaves absorbed photons of the red and blue spectrum of light waves, and repulsed the waves of the green spectrum. The waves of light — this bouquet of green leaves — reached the Olive at the speed of light. And since speed existed, then distance existed as well, and if there was distance, there was time.

The Olive considered what time meant. It felt at the very center of the present, since it was at the heart of its own calculations.

The same phenomenon occurs when an astronomer observes a star. He is not really watching the star shine; he is seeing the glow that has taken light-years to reach Earth. The astronomer does not observe the star in the present, but only the light of the past.

While the scientist calculates the time between a star and Earth in light-years, the Olive measured the time that separated it from the young tree in microseconds.

The Olive was living at the very crest of the present, and the emotion at seeing the olive grove wasting away in the past was a real one. Its reflections on the young tree were only an exercise, for this was the theorem: the Olive, pedunculated at the end of its branch, cursed the Patriarchal Olive Tree.

The Patriarchal Tree had a soul. It considered itself the *Living Encyclopedia of the Mediterranean* — nothing less. What smugness! Here was a presumptuous tree that dreamed of cataloguing all the floral motifs of the universal history of art and replacing them with the spear-shaped outline of its own leaf. Its roots scoured the soil in search of the workshops of Hephaistos the

Lame. Its branches watched the sky in hopes of spotting Hermes guided in his flight by the olive-wood caduceus. It spent years telling itself stories about the most beautiful legends and glorious battles of Antiquity. What's more, the Patriarchal Tree considered its fruits to be nothing more than droppings.

Obviously, Antiquity was mistaken. The olive tree did not deserve to be the symbol of goodness, idealism and peace. The tree might have been perfect back when it grew in the gardens of Olympus, but ever since it came down to earth, it had been the root of all evil, illness, crime and war. The most celebrated fratricides, the most furious ambition, the darkest carnal passions, the deadliest disobedience and the vilest perversion had been breathed into man by a toxin as fine as dust: the noxious pollen of the olive tree. Pandora, that woman fashioned by Hephaistos the Hideous (not to mention Lame), was sent down to earth by Zeus. She carried a box filled with pollen that the "Father of the Gods" himself had gathered from the twelve saplings of the sacred stump. When the box was opened, humanity was contaminated. And so began the history of the Mediterranean!

The Patriarchal Tree considered its fruits to be nothing more than droppings.

The Olive was a dropping. Its peduncle held it to a branch between earth and sky. It had been receiving a parsimonious ration of life-giving sap for more than a half century. God, was it old! And God, was it ugly!

Its pit, once as hard as Carrara marble, had gone rotten. A slight pressure of the index finger and the thumb and it would be crushed, like the turd of a fledgling. The firm, smooth, savory pulp had wasted away. Nothing was left but a fine film of black skin stretched pitifully over the viscous seed, the way a tattered overcoat is wrapped around a beggar sleeping on the pavement. There was still something between the endocarp and the epicarp, but it was sticky, rancid and difficult to identify. And after a half century under the Sicilian sun, it was highly poisonous!

Once, the Olive had been a magnificent, generous fruit. Enormous, fleshy, with round, oiled curves enough to make the half dozen unbuttoned boys with shaved heads salivate every time they came to admire it, this wonder of wonders. Their mouths gaped as wide as the dome of St. Peter's in Rome and let out *OOHs* and *AAHs* when the wind lifted the leaves, revealing the naked fruit. In their pockets, using the holes designed for just such a purpose, their hands kneaded their not yet virile members and their little sacs like walnut shells.

The mischievous gang watched the Olive with *eyes that undress a woman* . . . The Olive was much more than just an olive! It was full-bodied and languid on its branch. It was dressed in leaves that rustled in the breeze like whispering underthings, heavy with the fragrance of living things.

The Olive stirred the hearts of these Sicilian urchins. It awoke an irrepressible desire, the need to stroke it with the fingertips, then run off madly, shouting, "I touched it! I touched it! I touched it!" In the imaginations of those Latin rascals, the Olive reminded them of the harmony of a big breast they could breathe in and palpate and tickle without risking a resounding slap followed by imprecations in dialect. But all the diabolical ingenuity of that troop of shaved heads never succeeded in plucking the fruit from its tree. The Olive was impregnable. It was impossible to knock it off with a stick, and dangerous to climb onto the branch that extended over the edge of the cliff, which would have broken away.

Every afternoon, the swarm of urchins came up with a new trick to knock the fruit out of its tree. After every stinging failure — for all failures sting — exasperated, furious, they would throw themselves on the grass, and eat dirt, and punch each other in the head. They decided that the one who exhibited the most bruises would be responsible for their lack of success. Which would earn him a second round of punishment.

After the thrashing, bent double and aching, they would fall asleep in a heap at the foot of the Patriarchal Tree. They would snort and sniff whenever ants crawled into their nostrils. They looked like a litter of kittens.

After their nap, they would lick the most angry-looking of their contusions, clean their earth-stained teeth with twigs and pick off the scabs of blackish blood that were a permanent feature of their knees, elbows and heads. Then they would go streaming down the hillside, promising to return the next day with a new trick. They would scandalize the name of the *Santa Madonna,* those little Garibaldis!

In the days of its plenitude, the Olive was the finest fruit of the Mediterranean. The best of the *lucques,* ready to yield up an oil as yellow as gold, softer than skin, with a masterful taste that had perfumed the Mediterranean for millennia.

The Patriarchal Tree and the Olive were eternal antagonists. The tree had hidden the superb fruit and made it invisible to the pickers and impossible to glean by the indigent. Once, the Olive had wanted to be a rare and glorious fruit. And it had been, for a season . . . But now it was a dropping so disgusting that even the worms and grubs disdained it!

The Olive was a prisoner of the Patriarchal Tree. Chained by its peduncle, it cursed the landscape, this prison cell of incomparable beauty and infernal luminosity.

Between the Patriarchal Tree and the Olive, between olive trees and olives, there had never been anything but the tyranny of the trees and the martyrdom of the fruit.

Among the sounds and movements of the grove, a sensitive ear could pick out a plaintive drawing in of breath that was heard as soon as light whitened the sky. It was a music of nature, the *sotto voce* of billions of pedunculated olives. This lament, in which was contained all the cries and sobs of the heart, fell silent at twilight, after the apotheosis of suffering brought by the afternoon, when the light cuts deepest and the fruit receives alkaloid torn from the earth. The many voices of the olives were ineffable in their beauty and perfection, for they were a true *opera della Natura*.

Allow me this analogy.

How could we not think back to the Hebrew captives, constrained to labor on the banks of the Euphrates, as described by the librettist Solera? How could we not hear the celebrated *Va pensiero* by the patriotic maestro Giuseppe Verdi? The chorus of pedunculated olives and the chorus of enslaved Hebrews are both hymns heavy with the ordeal of sorrow, with hope and emotion that burn in memory and lift up the soul.

Hear these slaves without a homeland who cry out under the yoke of Babylon. Imagine the elegy of the olives of Sicily . . . And the weeping narrator!

Va, pensiero, sull'ali dorate;
Va, ti posa sui clivi, sui colli,
Ove olezzano tepide e molli

L'aure dolci del suolo natal!
Del Giordano le rive saluta,
Di Sionne le torri atterrate . . .
Oh, mia patria si bella e perduta!

The Olive, by becoming as beautiful as an orange, wanted to outstrip the magnificence of the Patriarchal Tree. The Tree would never let it go. It needed it. The Olive was a warning, a living lesson that had intimidated domestic olives for decades.

The Olive began its sixtieth year of enslavement to its branch. And since the Patriarchal Tree, symbol and sire of the grove (every tree had sprung from its scions by cutting and layering), was beginning the second half of its twelfth century with firmness and vigor, the suffering of the vain little fruit seemed to be eternal.

Here is the hierarchy of things: the cruel and dominating sun stretching from one horizon to the other; the Great Patriarchal Tree, sire of the grove; the millions of olive trees in methodical rows; the billions of olives, as green as sickness and black as melancholy; and the sexagenarian Olive, shriveled and hideous, rotting, suffering and very much alive.

This architectonia would have gone on for centuries if it hadn't been for two young lovers who, without knowing it, were about to sabotage the entire well-oiled machine.

Milli Palme was the lover. He had a shaved head.

Sicilian boys had their heads shaved. The island's hygiene demanded it. That way, no one would be forced to see the sap of the pistachio trees, turning pearly in the African sun, caking the boys' hair. With their shaved heads, they would lie under the branches and count the drops of warm resin that fell onto their skulls: Plop . . . 1. Plop . . . 2. Plop . . . 3. Plop . . . 4. Plop . . . 5. Plop . . . 6. Plop . . . 7. Plop . . . 8. Plop . . . 9. Plop . . . 10. Plop . . . 11. Plop . . . 12. Plop . . . 13. Plop . . . 14. Plop . . . 15. Plop . . . 16. Plop . . . 17.

And later . . .

Plop . . . 29. Plop . . . 30. Plop . . . 31.

Milli Palme had given up the game some time ago, but his mother kept on with the head-shaving. The older the boy grew, the more frequent the razor. The poor kid's skull often bore marks. His overflowing, intrusive mamma refused to believe that her little angel from On High could one day become a mortal man. She couldn't imagine that those quick eyes, which she covered with fleshy kisses, could be capable of *the look that undresses a woman . . .*

Pina Di Vita was the other lover. She was the youngest daughter of a large family that worked the family business: olive groves. Even the lunatic uncle participated in the prosperity by designing allegorical machinery. His goal was to automate the harvest and rid the grove of the workers, who represented 68 percent of the oil's production costs.

In the Di Vita house, checks came raining down. And the passion for dividends brought in even more! In that singular atmosphere, overheated by filthy lucre and machination, Pina Di Vita could slip out without attracting attention, then return, her eyes sparkling, her hair disheveled and tangled with twigs, her lips fulfilled and her gait languid . . .

Pina Di Vita was a Mediterranean girl, silent and timid; love made her cry out for the first time. What a pleasure to see those slender bodies, accustomed to the desk and the prie-dieu, come together with such force, and employ volcanic impetuousness to undertake the most complicated contortions! After the storm passed, the young lovers, their bodies wearing pearls of sweat, starred with insects attracted by their moisture, gasped for breath like men and women on the threshold of death. All this took place on a blanket, at the foot of the Patriarchal Tree.

Milli Palme didn't like that tree. In fact, the whole countryside abhorred the Great Patriarchal Olive Tree.

Three generations of the Di Vita family had accumulated vast holdings by means of fraud. In the last century, during a time of great drought, Corrado Di Vita, the part-swindler, part-landowner ancestor, forced all the small landholders to convert to the cultivation of the olive. With false arguments, he provided the scions and proposed a financial arrangement for the seven years the young trees would need before they'd produce their first fruit. The entire countryside took to cultivating this new product.

Centuries-old peasant ways immediately began disappearing. Songs in dialect, traditional costumes, popular holidays and votive feasts, legends and even the nursery rhymes mothers sang to lull their children to sleep under their blankets — none of those things had any relation to the landscape now that it had totally changed its appearance. Even the old witches and the women who cast spells couldn't accomplish their sorcery. The light, the air, the earth, the smells, the colors, the physiognomy of the land, the power of plants and the malevolent gifts of certain viscera — this entire miniature, magic world had been transformed by the unexpected, massive and undesirable arrival of the olive tree.

When the trees began to produce, the ancestor Corrado Di Vita set ceilings on supply and demand. He became the absolute master of price fluctuation. And the prices did fluctuate! The landowners, often illiterate and already deep in debt, became overextended and were ruined. The poor had no choice but to give up their land and become tenant farmers, and to teach their sons to curse the olive and the family who had forced them to grow it.

Turning landowners into sharecroppers was a perverse machination. It minimized agricultural responsibility while creating an army of docile workers, tied to the earth and easy to oppress with threats of seizure and expulsion.

The Patriarchal Tree was a living allegory, the symbol of the runaway prosperity of the Di Vita family and the Third World existence of the rest of the population. On Sundays and holidays, in the squares and marketplaces and cafés, people would mutter:

When the Great Patriarchal Olive Tree falls, the Di Vita family will fall, too . . . And the land will return to those who love it and work it.

"*La terra è di cu la zappa, no di cu porta cappa*," they would say. "The land belongs to the one with the spade, not to the one with the cape on his back."

Milli Palme did not love Pina Di Vita. The lover did not love his mistress.

The girl wore a bracelet, from which a variety of charms dangled: a stiletto, an eye, a hand, a Doric column, a stylized sun with rays like daggers, a replica of Sicily with a diamond set in it, an olive tree, a spear-shaped leaf and an olive. On a chain around her neck she wore a superb *Trinacria,* the coat of arms of Sicily: a winged woman's head, coiffed with a serpent's tangle and surrounded by three legs, bent as if they were running. The eyes were cut from live coral. All that gold inflamed the young man's senses.

The *Trinacria* stank of the fetidness of poverty. Milli Palme knew that smell, for it filled his family's house. Every beam, every stone was steeped in it, from the foundations to the rafters. And the bracelet with its string of charms tasted of blood. The blood of a grandfather who'd died of sadness after having been so shamefully despoiled by Corrado Di Vita, her ancestor.

Can gold, unalterable, impervious to rust, invulnerable to air and water, carry smells and tastes? In young Milli Palme's understanding, bitter and crying nightly as he lay in his narrow bed because of his family's poverty, the answer was *Yes!* Her gold was damascened with blood, sweat and tears. Pina Di Vita wore the misery of three generations of the Palme family like a crown.

The boy didn't love the girl who cried out during pleasure, and he hated the Great Patriarchal Tree above his head.

Besides, the lover was not a great lover. He understood nothing of the sensations and mysteries that can arise when two bodies come together. He preferred playing soccer in the dust, or eating grilled lizards under the almond trees, to surrendering to chimerical enchantments. But adversity had made him grow up fast . . . And all that gold stamped with signs that Pina Di Vita wore with sovereign assurance on her wrist and heaving breast increased his manly vigor tenfold.

Milli Palme put aside his glossy paper images of Ferraris and Lamborghinis, Bugattis and Maseratis, and his collection of beetles mounted on corrugated cardboard to embark on a heartfelt but ridiculous project: between the panting and the embraces, the boy would kill the tree. Engraving love poems into the Patriarchal Tree's trunk, dazzling his lover in the process, Milli lacerated it down to the sapwood, all the way to the hardwood. Those endless poems were set off by flourishes, spirals and scrolls, garlands and complicated designs. As the days went by, the rusty blade chipped off sections of bark and made the splinters fly. As the days went by, the Great Patriarchal Tree weakened . . .

> When the Great Patriarchal Olive Tree falls, the Di Vita family will fall, too . . . And the land will return to those who love it and work it.

"When this cursed olive tree dies, I'll go to America," the bold young poet decided.

Pina Di Vita was too impressed by Milli Palme's zeal to suspect anything of her lover's irreversible designs. Her eyes were closed. She blew out a great stream of air through her mouth and nose and declared, "*La Madonna, that was good!*"

The Great Patriarchal Tree gave its first fruit under the flourishing occupation of the Arabs. They landed on the triangular island, bringing with them advanced agricultural techniques, dates, lemons, oranges, peaches, sugar, sherbets, cotton, silkworms, maps of the night sky, a new conception of the universe, new mathematical relationships, high-gloss ceramics, arabesques and Moslem fatalism.

The sire of the Great Patriarchal Tree was exhibited in a glass cage in the National Archaeological Museum in the capital. *Primo Oleastro* was engraved on a bronze plaque at the base of the glass. The tree had been fossilized by fumarole gases, petrified by volcanic composites and buried under a rain of ash and lava. A team of volcano specialists had discovered it in one of Mount Etna's solfataric crevasses as they were out prospecting on the cones, craters and chimneys. The tree was intact, with speckled leaves, their surface lined like fine porcelain.

Paleobotanical studies of pollen, particles and gases trapped in the wood, bark and roots proved that this was one of the first oleasters of Asia Minor brought to the island by Phoenician navigators. Tests confirmed that every olive tree — from Lisbon to the Aegean shores of Turkey, from Provence to the valley of the Nile — possessed the same DNA structure as the *Primo Oleastro*. The fossil on display at the National Archaeological Museum was the supreme, universal father of every *oleo europea* in the Mediterranean!

The *Primo Oleastro* and its offspring, the Patriarchal Tree, witnessed more than 2,700 years of invasion and occupation of Sicily. They watched the landings of Greeks, Carthaginians, Romans, Vandals, Byzantines, Arabs, Normans, Germans, the French of Anjou, the Spanish, the Austrians, the Bourbons of Naples, Garibaldi's Red Shirts, Cavour's government servants, Mussolini's Black Shirts and — during World War number 2 — the armed forces of the United States of America, accompanied by a handful of brave Canadian soldiers and a few battalions of square-headed Englishmen. These invaders trod Sicilian ground with their weaponry, political systems, religious practices, artistic and architectonic codes, taxes that enriched foreign governments — not to speak of the cartons of Lucky Strikes and Wrigley's chewing gum.

The chronology is enough to make your head spin! And the irony makes it spin twice as fast. Think of it! The Great Patriarchal Olive Tree, this living memory that knew every culture and every army, dying at the hand of a young islander, his blade and his poems! The

Great Patriarchal Tree was dying.

The sexagenarian Olive, seeing that its nightmare was about to end, addressed itself to the Patriarch. An olive can speak to its tree. A very rare event, but possible.

"You are dying, and your death will be without glory. But I can put a stop to your torment. Move my branch, my twig, my peduncle, my chain above these lovers. Place me just above them. When I give you the sign, break this cursed peduncle. I can't tell you any more, but your pain will cease the very next day. Your agony will be over the very next day."

"Who are you to speak to me this way? You're a seditious olive. You have no right to favors or clemency."

"Great Millenary Tree, break this cursed peduncle. Your agony will cease the very next day. Your pain will cease."

"And how will your deliverance spare me from torment?"

"Soon you will give up the ghost, and I, with you. For our species, your Majesty, it will be death without glory. For me, it will signal the end of a torment that has lasted long enough. I will gain much and you will lose everything. I will gain much and you will be left with nothing."

"And if I break your peduncle?"

"That is my business."

"That's not explanation enough."

"You know all there is to know. If you hold me back, we'll die together. You will die stupidly, and I, fulfilled."

"I am a sublime olive tree and you are just a dropping."

"I am not challenging your grandeur. I am not challenging your supremacy. It is true, I am just a dropping . . . But the fact is that you are going to die, and I can keep that from happening. Drop me over those lovers, and I promise I will spare you death . . . and, later, war!"

"War?"

"I will wait until your wounds heal. I will wait the years it will take for your vigor to return. And only then will I declare war on you."

"The Olive is incapable of warlike actions."

"The Great Olive Tree venerates war as a tragic and sublime activity that completes the perfection of humanity. War is at the origin of all things. War is the goddess of progress" (F. T. Marinetti).

"The Olive is a dropping."

"That can't be changed . . ."

"You are a dropping."

"At your service!"

"Do you not smell the stink of peace?" (Gabriele D'Annunzio).

"I smell only the stink of droppings."

"Is war the world's only hygiene?" (F. T. Marinetti).

"I'll always be a dropping."

"I have contempt for droppings. And I am opposed to the easy life" (Benito Mussolini).

"Dictatorship is the most complete form of jealousy" (Curzio Malaparte).

"I seek to live in danger" (Benito Mussolini).

"Break the peduncle and I promise you every peril."

By now, the Olive was hanging over the lovers. Freed from its foliage, it warmed itself in the sun. It wanted to reach the temperature of the human body. Below, the boy carved away at the trunk under the pretext of love and romance. Close by him, the girl was sleeping on the blanket. Her black skirt was pushed up to her hips. Her buttocks, admirable in their roundness, shone in the sunlight like a pair of Byzantine domes ornamented by pink glass mosaic. The Olive was heating up. The pact was sealed. The Patriarchal Tree, urged on by promises of war, was about to snap the peduncle.

The olive grove was confused. The trees feared a terrible future. The pact between the Great Patriarch and a single, wrinkled Olive was something that simply wasn't done. The tree had been excited by specious reasoning, delirious and dying as it was. Besides, a sovereign should not have truck with droppings!

Trees and olives have always been enemies. The bargaining only served to intensify the animosity. A strange chorus arose from the grove. The dose of alkaloids had been doubled. Never had a grove given such fine fruit, a harvest unequaled in the annals of Mediterranean oleiculture.

"Farewell, olives, my clamoring sisters . . ."

"It's time to get it over with!"

"I promise you death and humiliation for all eternity."

The stem snapped. The Olive quit the tree. It landed on a dome of sun-splashed flesh. Pina Di Vita was dozing. She didn't feel that fleshy, smooth, warm thing alight on her, right there, which, following the laws of gravity, then slipped into the cleft that separates that part of the anatomy into two model sections. That fleshy bit of life slid forward and found itself face to face with her wet vulva, still quivering. The oily Olive found refuge there.

Pina Di Vita opened her eyes. The sounds and movements of nature flowed above her. Insects scratched and rattled all around. Their ribbed, translucent wings sparkled for a fraction of a second when they turned at a certain angle to the sun, and the beating of all those membranes made the air thrum. Scents and perfumes cascaded down to her: almond, lemon and orange trees mixed with mint, black currant, magnolia and myrrh, and these odors made a chaotic, stubborn bouquet. Her face pressed against the grass, Pina Di Vita gazed through the twigs and yellow flowers at the olive trees, with their twisted trunks and foliage so like lace woven from silver thread.

"A sea of trees," she said aloud.

The lover turned his head slowly towards his beloved. He buried his knife in the tree, emboldened by fresh enthusiasm. He moved to her side, settled in, caressed and mounted her. Milli Palme and Pina Di Vita made love between two fires: the impudent sun above, and the molten, sulphurous convulsions of Etna's lair below.

The lovers hadn't noticed that a light olive purée was blocking the entry to her vagina. They never knew that this soft paste had been driven inside Pina by Milli's erection, and later, had mingled with his seed. The light exploded in silence against their streaming, naked bodies that glowed at the foot of the Great Patriarchal Olive Tree. The bright reflections could be seen from afar, moving to the rhythm of the ardent passion of their lovemaking. Those lights were like shapeless mirrors hung from a branch with wires, playthings of the wind. They were like a luminous signal, a sentinel who, from his position on the promontory, must warn his superiors of the imminent movements of the troops.

At least, that's the way Signore Di Vita interpreted those mirror-like reflections that seemed to go on and on as he stood at his large office window.

"The signal . . . the signal . . . the signal," he murmured.

Signore Di Vita had collaborated in the landing of the American army in Sicily during World War number 2. Already, back then, he was a respectable young man with a bright future within the local hierarchy. The landing was right up his alley! Using men armed with lamps at night, and large mirrors during the day, he developed a network of semaphore signals that outlined a wide bay, hidden by mountains, a secret to all but the local population. Then, with the artifice of a dozen gardeners, he transformed this inhospitable ground into a secure landing zone, ready to receive the heavy, motorized army of the United States of America. Thousands of soldiers and hundreds of armored vehicles, guided by diurnal and nocturnal signals, landed in Sicily on this carefully landscaped beach, as welcoming and pleasant as any mainland resort. Relaxation and serenity were the order of the day, all in a Homeric setting. Barefoot in the sand, the soldiers smoked their cigarettes, chatted and drank bottles of the local wine in a calm atmosphere that was downright insolent, considering the atrocities taking place elsewhere in Europe. Their tanks were decorated with geraniums and hydrangeas; they caught magnificent tuna with the help of underwater grenades; they jumped into the sea, naked; they played cards; they yawned and sunbathed, waiting for their orders, which were bogged down in endless negotiations among Washington, London and the Little Italy district in New York.

Signore Di Vita was not a great patriot. He was a
chauvinist when it came to local rivalries, and an oppor-
tunist as far as Rome was concerned. He couldn't have
cared less about the liberation of Rome! He hated the far-
off capital. It levied taxes, imposed the cult of efficiency,
machinery and war, dictated the fashion of black shirts
and praised *the quest for sensation* celebrated by a bunch of
decadent poets. From Rome, all the contempt and arrogance of the industrial northern cities converged on the
south. Signore Di Vita was among those, and they were
numerous, who wanted Sicily to become the forty-ninth
state of the United States of America. With crude, black
brushstrokes, the boldest of them took to painting the
figure 49 on the stuccoed fountains and walls of government buildings. After a few vague suggestions and the
Allied victory, Washington showed no further interest
in this land of bandits and obscure clans, where every
vice was represented. The Sicilians, masters in the art of
watching their destiny slip between their fingers, were
left with a bitter taste in their mouths. Signore Di Vita,
despite American decorations and Italian honors, had to
choke back his frustration — a frustration that did not
lessen with the passing years!

Sitting at his desk, in the cool of his office, Signore Di
Vita watched the reflections through his large window.

"The signal," he muttered to himself. "The signal . . . the signal."

His mind was subject to certain aberrations whenever he stared at the sparkling of bright lights. Leftover trauma from the war, so it would seem. Oftentimes, on Sunday, during Mass, Signora Di Vita could be seen slapping her husband as his wide, moist eyes lost focus at the sight of the ciborium, chalice, censer or any other object that might shine and sway in the dark chancel. The blows rang out in the ogival nave and the faithful laughed happily. One day, Father Di Berio fell out of the pulpit and broke his bones, all with a smile!

Signore Di Vita recalled those strategic signals from another time, even if several decades had buried the glorious episode of the landing.

"The signal . . . the signal . . . the signal," he muttered.

He measured the intensity, calculated the cadence, counted the intervals and looked for some relationship as he drank down great swallows of wine. Then, suddenly, he dropped his pen on a mountain of scribbled papers.

"What's behind those signals? And why at the foot of my millenary Patriarchal Tree?"

The escarpment was barely visible, and the Great Olive Tree could not be seen, but the reflections of light came from that direction . . . Yes, right there!

Signore Di Vita was in the presence of a warning,

presaging a new and crushing stroke of fate. And in the face of a crushing stroke of fate, a man must remain stoic. That was how people here warded off surprises, both good and bad, that in the end were simply disturbances, mortally complicated and apt to keep a man from dreaming.

He opened a drawer, produced a pair of binoculars he'd stolen from General Patton, then took up his position in front of the window.

"Why there, on the promontory where my Patriarchal Tree lives?" he cried out a second time.

Crisply, Signore Di Vita raised his binoculars to his eyes in imitation of the American officers whom, in his younger days, he'd admired for their haughty indolence, made even more sophisticated by their chewing gum. The lovers shone. Two little balls of fire. Signore Di Vita, the father, watched Pina Di Vita, his daughter, cry out, "*La Madonna,* that was good!"

The little donkey was struggling. The poor animal was climbing the final stretch of the path leading to the Patriarchal Tree. Flies and wasps buzzed around its head, its muzzle whitened with slaver that baked in the sun. The Pizzi brothers followed behind, fanning themselves with their caps. Their shirts were soaked. When they reached the tree, they freed the donkey from the pack that was practically crushing its ribs. The animal was carrying a curious load: fifty liters of water, asphalt, plaster, manure, petroleum jelly, bluish powdered lava, pozzolana, some bottles of aspirin, corn flour, vitamins and mineral salts, sulphur, veal scallopini, spaghetti, tomatoes, eggplants, a loaf of bread, rounds of cheese, olives, olive oil, a magnum of anisette, several bottles of wine, a gas stove and its accompanying canister, pots and pans, a drainer, a cast-iron kettle, plates and cutlery, an ax, a spade, a shovel, a hoe, a rake, a pair of clippers, a pruning instrument, a set of knives, a hook, a clamp, files, tongs, chisels, steel line, a pail . . .

Poor little donkey. The brothers washed it down to cleanse it of the dried slaver and dust. Then they rubbed its nose and tongue with anisette. The drunken, stumbling donkey was completely terrorized.

The Pizzi brothers were celebrated cultivators of the olive, true masters. Even if the trees they nurtured didn't belong to them. Even if the land they loved wasn't theirs. They were the best!

The Pizzi brothers began to sing:

Semu di terra, e a la terra a tutt'uri
La sorti nostra nni chiama e nni voli:
La terra assuppa li nostri suduri,
Vita uni duna e cunvorta lu cori.

(We belong to the land, and to the land
Our fate calls us, it is our destiny:
The land is watered with our sweat,
It comforts and gladdens our hearts.)

Signore Di Vita had spent good money bringing in the brothers from their poor, back-country hamlet. They were expensive. Very expensive! Yet the payment the Pizzi brothers asked for was not very high; their demands were actually quite modest. The donkey was the problem! The animal alone demanded a salary equivalent to that of ten field-workers for a whole year — nothing less!

"Take it or leave it," one of the brothers declared.

"It's all three, or none," the other brother chimed in.

The argument of the two olive experts ran something like this.

"Signore Di Vita, my brother and I are the best because we are antiques. Our knowledge is archaic because the love and respect for the trade have come to us from another time. We are old, immensely old! And we must stay that way . . . Which is very hard these days, I'm sure you'll agree! Thanks to the donkey, we are much older than we are in reality. Without our donkey, we'd be modern! And no one can cultivate olive trees if they're modern. Especially if the tree is the famous millenary Patriarchal Tree!"

"That's exactly the way it is," said the other brother, saluting this obvious truth made even more obvious by rhetorical flourish. "So if you want us to save your millenary Olive Tree, we'll need three checks. One for him, one for me and the third for the donkey."

"Write a check to a donkey!" Signore Di Vita cried.

"A check for the donkey. The donkey has enormous responsibilities, and he should be paid accordingly. You will make the check out to Tito Asino. That's the name under which he accumulates his interest at the bank."

"The donkey has a bank account?" Di Vita cried out once more.

"Of course! You understand, my brother and I are poor field-workers. We travel the roads of Sicily in search of a crust of bread! But him, the one with four feet, he's got an organized mind — he's even rich! And benevolent, to boot! He advances us money if the harvests are lean, or when the taxman bleeds us to death."

"Sometimes, we forget to file our returns," the other brother admitted.

"But I can't very well make a check out to a donkey!"

"Signore Di Vita, Tito Asino is a hard-working, coura-geous animal. This donkey will accept the difficult, arduous tasks involved in work in the fields without so much as a word of complaint. But what can you do, Tito is a donkey, and a donkey he will stay. The Good Lord wanted him that way! We are his guardians, having received his benediction. And the Lord's, too, of course. You understand our conditions. If you accept, you will write three checks, and everything will be settled."

"Three checks, and everything will be settled," the other brother echoed.

"This damned island!" the owner of the Patriarchal Tree muttered.

Di Vita had no choice! Committed fatalist that he was, seeing signs left and right, he was convinced that if his millenary Patriarchal Tree fell, his fortune and prosperity would soon follow suit. The millenary Tree had to live, and its owner would pay the price. The Pizzi brothers knew it. To claim that the donkey knew it, too, forgive me if I have my doubts! A donkey is a donkey is a donkey, and that's the way the Good Lord wanted him.

The Pizzi brothers liked to think that the civil servants from the tax department were asses, too, but in a different way. Something that had nothing to do with the will of God.

These masters of the olive got down to work. They walked circles around the tree. They gesticulated and fulminated against the earth, the sky and the sun. Despite Signore Di Vita's completely accurate and often repeated descriptions, the Pizzi brothers could not have imagined a more devastating scene: the Patriarchal Tree stripped of its bark, lacerated down to its core, the ground covered with wood chips.

"This is not the work of a madman. It is the considered and well-planned act of an individual in full possession of his faculties," the first brother stated.

"The boy wanted to kill the Patriarchal Tree and cause the ruin of the Di Vita family," the second brother concluded.

The Pizzi brothers were well aware of the ignoble saga of the Di Vita family, and how quickly it had become rich and powerful. Their heads spun when they considered the raw courage the young teenager had shown. But where had the boy gone to? they wondered.

"America," Signore Di Vita replied.

The Patriarchal Tree was going to die. They had better move fast. The olive-cultivating brothers gathered up the wood chips and mixed them with the manure, aspirin, bluish lava, pozzolana, asphalt, plenty of corn flour, plaster, vitamins, mineral salts, petroleum jelly and twenty liters of water. They boiled the preparation in the big cast-iron kettle with a few tomatoes, sulphur and a liter of pastis until the mixture turned viscous. Next they let it cool.

The Pizzi brothers took time out to read the inscriptions and admire the precise work evident in the engraved letters, the ornamentation, masks, scrolls and flourishes. Then they covered everything over with a smooth layer of the soft, sticky, pungent mixture. Good craftsmen that they were, the master olive-cultivators recognized the patience and devotion that characterize the artist who truly loves his trade. They were in a state of amazement. They pictured the young man engraving these romantic daydreams and carving the ornamentation in order to kill the Patriarchal Tree and bring down the Di Vita family. Emotion overcame the brothers, and that was saying a lot, considering their simple, earth-bound natures. At the foot of the millenary Tree, the Pizzi brothers spoke in low tones, stroked the chiseled out figures and wept.

"But where is he? Where is the great artist?"

Three times a day, they removed the ointment and applied a fresh coat. Three times a day, the Pizzi brothers reread the poems, stroked the same engraved ornamentation and wept fresh tears. After the fresh coat and further lamentations, they sat down to a meal of spaghetti with tomato sauce and veal scallopini, they drank their wine, meditated on the physiognomy of the young poet and recited bits of verse that had come to rest in their memories. In the evening, they traveled down to the luxurious Di Vita manor, where a room had been prepared for them in the barn. The next day, they went back to care for the tree with a new stock of materials. Poor little donkey!

After a few days' work, the master olive-cultivators knew all of Milli Palme's poetry. They collected the poems in the *Anthology for Killing a Millenary Patriarchal Olive Tree,* a collection that lived in their minds. Every morning and every evening, whenever the donkey refused to budge, they would whisper a few verses into its ear. And the stubborn animal would start trotting along briskly, as if the devil were pulling on its tail!

Between pasta with tomato sauce and coats of balm, the Pizzi brothers would put on a show. While one recited excerpts from the *Anthology,* the other, lying in the grass, a twig between his teeth and a wine glass in his hand, would weep. Then they would switch roles. The first actor would stretch out, drink his wine and try not to dissolve in tears before the moving performance of his brother, whose eyes were still wet.

They added critical commentary: this passage should be more languorous, while the other one lacked fire, and here, don't forget to whimper a little . . .

The escarpment became a theater: a protagonist, a rigorous text, the sun, a millenary olive tree (instigator of all intrigue), with the olive grove serving as the set. All that was missing was the semicircle dug out of the tuff and the antique masks fitted with mouthpieces.

The treatment took fifteen days. On the sixteenth, the owner of the tree was invited to inspect the results of the Pizzi brothers' care and put his name to the three checks.

"No! Not with the truck. The Tree is still weak, and all that machine noise might traumatize it," one of the brothers pointed out.

"You'll have to go on donkeyback. Olive trees love donkeys," the other brother put in.

The three men fanned themselves with their hats: two caps and a local Panama. The Pizzi brothers sang from the *Anthology for Killing a Millenary Patriarchal Olive Tree,* which they adapted to various popular melodies, while Signore Di Vita admired the little donkey's agility and vivacity.

"What makes him run like that? It's like the devil's pulling his tail!"

"Tito Asino doesn't like poets. Especially poets who assault olive trees," one of the brothers answered.

"Tito only likes checks," the other chimed in.

Signore Di Vita was satisfied. The prosperity of the family was saved. The Patriarchal Olive Tree would heal. He could see the new shoots at the ends of the branches. The trunk was plastered with a mortar of asphalt and volcanic dust kept in place by a copper sleeve. Potassium and mineral salt lozenges lay on the ground by the hundreds.

"You'll need to water the ground every Sunday morning until the lozenges disappear," a brother said.

"The Tree will survive, but it will bear scars," the other added.

"Scars!" Signore Di Vita exclaimed. "But there are scars everywhere! Sicily is covered with scars . . . A few more, a few less, what's the difference? When you consider the condition this place is in . . ."

"That's exactly right," the Pizzi brothers agreed.

Does not the Sicilian live with scars?

Scars of every shape and every origin! Greek temples, Roman aqueducts, Byzantine vaults, Arab minarets, Norman cathedrals, baroque Spanish palaces, fascist cubes and American bombs have marked the face of the island, the way Greek sophism, Roman rationality, Moslem fatalism, French hypocrisy, Spanish vanity and Neapolitan skulduggery have sculpted the fundamental traits of the Sicilian soul through centuries of historical division.

The glaring remains of ancient civilizations have stigmatized Sicily. But the Sicilian has stopped seeing them. He has forgotten his own stories. All those soporific old stones make the islander yawn if he contemplates them for too long . . .

The Sicilian is a living island on another island, triangular in shape, stuck in the middle of the Mediterranean Sea. His scars have become the magnificent, triumphant extension of a perpetual, dreamlike inertia!

The Patriarchal Tree would live, and Signore Di Vita would cover up the whole business with a thick layer of dust, and sleep . . . Sleep a sleep so deep it would merge into nothingness.

"Gentlemen, you have worked a miracle. You have saved my Great Patriarchal Tree. Let us go back to the house. I'll settle up for what I owe you, and we'll sit down to a good meal."

"No. Pay us now. We have a train to catch. We have work elsewhere," one of the brothers replied.

"Pay you here? Now?"

"Yes. Here. Now."

Signore Di Vita took out his checkbook and made out three checks.

"Pardon me, but you've made a mistake in the amount."

"I took the liberty of adding a bonus for a job well done. No one can say that I cut corners!"

"Signore Di Vita, we won't accept your bonus. And when I say 'we,' I include the donkey, of course."

"You don't want my bonus? Field-workers who turn up their noses at money — now, that's a first!"

"There's a first time for everything."

The Pizzi brothers' tone, their independence, their refusal to take his bonus — all that irritated the owner of the Patriarchal Tree. He scribbled out three checks.

"Signore Di Vita, what became of the artist?" one brother asked.

"What artist?"

"The poet!"

"What poet?"

"The boy who wanted to kill the millenary Patriarchal Olive Tree."

"Ah, that madman! I didn't know he was an artist or a poet. The sea took him."

"The sea? May God bless him!"

Simultaneously, the three men crossed themselves, though Signore Di Vita's sign was that of the impostor. He confused *Sanctus Spiritus* with *Spiritus Sanctus,* and the other way around.

"The sea . . . She brings us great misfortune and carries away our greatest artists. To America, I suppose?" the other brother asked.

"Yes, of course, America," said the Olive Tree's owner.

"*Amèrica!*" the second brother exclaimed.

The Sicilian bears no love for the sea. All great calamities are carried on her breast: conquering armies, the plague, the sirocco, taxes and new inventions that are to be regarded with such suspicion. On that same sea, whole families have departed Sicily for Canada and the

United States, leaving behind them empty villages and whimpering relations.

At one point, the sea was taking everyone! It was commonplace for an adventurous young man to head for the bakery to buy a loaf of bread, with a few *lira* in his pocket — or so he'd say — and then disappear. "The sea took him," people would conclude.

A few decades later, the young man would return. He had Americanized his name: Giuseppe had become Joe, and Francesco, Frank. He wore a mustache and spoke another language. He smoked Winstons at the wheel of a long, chrome-plated automobile. Proudly, he showed off his woman, a young American taller than he was, who talked through her nose, a blonde, of course, with a painted face, wrapped as tight as a sausage, tottering around on her high heels. Prodigal America returning to the family home! A classic scene! His mother, when she recognized her "new" son, vociferated in the name of all the Saints on High as she beat him with the first blunt object she could find — usually a frying pan, since the Sicilian *mamma* is always busy in the kitchen.

"The sea takes you," people would say, "and *mamma* takes you back."

The American girl would wait outside, terrorized by the mother's weeping and wailing — the very voice of the earth — and totally taken aback by the son's tears and sobs. She would begin to melt in the haughty sun while, from out of the woodwork, a dozen languorous men, hands in their pockets, cigarettes hanging from their lips, with bedroom eyes, turned circles around her, their silence intolerable and their impassiveness presumptuous. That was the limit! She'd scarcely set foot on the island, and already the poor girl was cursing its caustic light, fossilized society and backward peasants. The tall blonde had the distinct feeling that she was neither at the right time, nor in the right place . . . A common enough sensation in Sicily!

Milli Palme had disappeared. In the countryside, people said, "The sea took him." There was something noble about America. No sense worrying, for he would return. A Sicilian always returned on the waves that bore him away — to *mamma,* to the land — even if it meant getting bonked on the head with a frying pan!

One day, in the arid grazing lands of the back country, a shepherd discovered the body of a teenaged boy under a mound of stones. The police launched an inquiry. It would not be easy: the head, hands and feet of the young man had been cut off. The carabinieri scoured the region, hoping to gather the missing extremities and head. Their search was in vain. The police were faced with a body they could not identify. They were about to close the investigation when they decided to make one last attempt to break the case. The Prefect summoned the parents whose son had been "taken by the sea."

"Who knows," he said to himself, "maybe Milli Palme isn't in America. Perhaps he's here in the basement, in the morgue."

The body was unveiled to the parents. They crossed themselves at the sight of the unfortunate victim.

"Take a good look at this body. Is it your son, Milli Palme?"

"No," Signore and Signora Palme answered forcefully.

"Are you sure? Look at him carefully. Take your time. Are you absolutely sure that this boy is not your son?"

"Sir, this woman is the mother of Milli Palme. And I am his father. And you, you represent justice. That's good. Everything is as it should be, so let's leave it that way. If I maintain that this is not Milli Palme's body, then it's not Milli Palme's body. Again, everything is as it should be, so let's leave it that way. Please do not insist, for I might interpret your insistence as a form of doubt. I know who my sons are. If there is a son whose existence I know nothing of, then I am left wearing the horns. And that is a matter which no longer concerns the Ministry of Justice, but which concerns us. You and I, as men. Do you understand what I'm saying?"

The Prefect sent them away. The parents were lying. The headless, amputated body was indeed that of Milli, their son. But to admit that to an outsider, a representative of the Ministry of Justice from Rome, would have complicated things terribly, and forever. Signore and Signora Palme had a right to their inertia, their luxurious form of surrender. They had a right to the kind of sleep that makes love with nothingness . . .

Sleep follows fatigue. The Sicilian is an extenuated being. The 2,700 years of military, political, artistic and religious occupation, and innovations of all kinds, have exhausted him. Apprehension wraps him in a killing embrace. As do surprises. Rome and her ministries, the puppet theater, suspicion and collusion, bombs and killings, plots and taxes, the debris of past civilizations every time you plant a hoe in the ground, historical atavism, immigration, steeple bells in the wind, youth turning to old age, drinking wine, olive oil, *talking about women,* playing cards, love, land, sea, sun, sirocco — they are stones in the boot of the Sicilian.

Milli Palme's body looked like a calf hanging in a butcher shop window. How could a person live with such a tragedy? How could a Mediterranean mother mourn her son when he had no hands to receive her last embrace, no face to be moistened by a storm of tears and kisses? How could his body lie in an open coffin underneath the chapel vault? How could he be presented to the merciful Lord? The body had been arranged according to the rules of a dark art, and that, everyone knew. The investigation would have dragged on, and much ink would have been spilled. And spilled ink exhausts the Sicilian soul!

So Milli Palme was in America. His parents imagined him there. Signore Di Vita found that scenario to his liking, too. The inhabitants of the island all agreed: Milli Palme had gone to America. And he was a thousand times better off there than in Sicily, in the basement of the police station!

Would the prophecy of the wrinkled Olive come true?

In water, wind and air, the Patriarchal Tree sought out the premonitions of war. The tree had sunk into long and useless speculation, and now it began to imagine strategies, each one more far-fetched than the last. His Majesty was turning decadent and senile. No more was the Patriarchal Tree the monolithic guidepost, the living heraldic ornament, the very breath of the grove's prosperity and felicity. It had become a worthless old man who still commanded respect, even if he did exhibit unfortunate signs of catatonia.

The other olive trees were clearly irritated. In the center of the grove stood a Doric temple. It had been erected by the imaginative power of the trees. On the frieze were inscribed the final words that the sexagenarian Olive — the dropping — had spoken to the

Great Patriarch: *I promise you death and humiliation for all eternity.* Inside, in the *naos,* in the spot normally occupied by the deified statue, was a perfect and very impressive copy of the Great Patriarch — upside down, with the branches pointing down and the roots up towards the coffered ceiling. Who would have thought that such a farce was possible? And the senile old Tree didn't notice a thing!

Pina Di Vita had no idea where she was. The mansion, built during the domination of Very Catholic Spain, looked like a giant *cassata siciliana.* It had been ruined by decades of neglect, three earthquakes and the bombs accidentally dropped by a young American pilot during that cursed World War number 2. An entire wing of the building was nothing more than a pile of gravel, stones and split timbers covered by flowering bougainvillea, acanthus and wild fennel with its bittersweet perfume. Battalions of scorpions, chameleons, toads, lizards, vipers and beetles appreciated the coolness of the ruins.

The other section, despite the bombing and neglect, remained inhabitable, shored up by a complicated criss-cross of scaffolding. The foundations oozed greenish slime, the roof beams stank of rancid oil, and the façade had lost all its stonework. The mansion was surrounded by a large garden, fruit trees, a row of laurel bushes, a plank shelter where guinea fowl lived and, a bit farther on, a pool, the domain of little animals that slithered and swam, jumped and crawled. It was actually a very lovely country dwelling!

Why were there so many balconies? Sicilian baroque had turned the balcony into something sophisticated, autonomous, airborne, a free space floating between the universe within and the world without. The Sicilian balcony acted as a loge; it allowed a person to apprehend all the tumultuous, cultural theatricality of life below, in the street. The balcony, for those who know how to read the signs, is an extraordinary blind for watching gestures, glances, tones of voice, silences and other details that can betray and unmask the hypertrophy of Sicilian ways of being.

On the façade of the mansion there were sixteen balconies, all decorated with luxurious, swelling ironwork and supported by corbels of the most extravagant design.

Why all those balconies, since there was neither noisy street nor teeming life, and no suspicion to feed this fearful need for the cloak of detail? Why so many balconies? To listen to the strident wings of the cicadas in the sea of olive trees, at the hour when the vipers crawl out?

There was another curiosity: a sundial surrounded by pale heraldic animals on a blistered wall, underneath the stairway in the main entryway. A sundial in perpetual darkness! What kind of idea was that?

Two suspicious, taciturn, cowardly men prowled the ruins, rifles slung over their shoulders, barrels pointing at the earth, while two humpbacked old women dressed in black watched over their pregnant young charge. Pina Di Vita called them the *sorelle cammelle* — the camel sisters. The nickname was the product of a flash of poetic inspiration: the old women were, in fact, sisters who, when they worked together in the garden, backs bent, looked exactly like a black camel. The camel effect grew stronger the closer you drew, when you noticed the hairs around their toothless mouths.

Few words were spoken in that house. The men didn't open their mouths because "it" didn't concern them, and the two humpbacked moralists stared at their young charge in silence as if she were the most sullied of sinners.

Few words were spoken, but Pina Di Vita could interpret the signs: in isolation, among the ruins, sheltered from malicious gossip, she would live out her pregnancy and whelp her bastard. And in a big hole among the laurels, a hole tended daily by the two men, her newborn would be buried with neither ceremony nor liturgy. The bastard would be wrapped in a sheet, placed at the bottom of the pit with a Bible and a crucifix, shovelfuls of dirt would be thrown on it to stifle its cries, a young laurel bush would be planted on the spot — a few whacks with the shovel on the mound of earth, and water liberally. The orthodoxy of the two cohorts would permit the infanticide.

Pina Di Vita translated all these signs. She gazed at the laurels; every bush seemed to have been planted at a different time. She contemplated the gaping hole. A monster that waited, its jaws wide, for its human fodder before disappearing back to the bowels of the earth, its domain. The girl was going to feed that monster with the fruit of her womb, as generations of poor girls before her had done. That she knew. And she would strive to do it well, in total abnegation.

Pina Di Vita found herself gasping for breath. Something heavy hung in the air. An authority stronger than Catholicism in its homogeneity and its hold, more earthbound and Sicilian in its essence: the century-old island ways.

"Under every laurel lies a Bible, a cross and a little set of tiny white bones," the girl said out loud. "The laurels have long roots that keep the bastards of poor unfortunates like me well anchored in the earth. I'm lost in this sea of olive trees where not a single sound strikes the ear, where no campanile embellishes the horizon and no human hand seems to work the land. Olive trees quicken the taste for death . . . All this melancholy beneath that cursed sun."

Pina Di Vita had her room upstairs. An immense oval salon inhabited by chubby *putti* who were busy disporting themselves, turning somersaults and quivering on the cornices, molding and pediments. But the layer of filth built up over decades of neglect had denatured these plump, fleshy cherubim. What a sad sight! It was enough to make you wonder whether these round-cheeked little angels truly belonged to the hierarchy of the Most High, or whether they weren't secretly sweating mortadella instead.

The ceiling — zenithal, elliptical, lapis-lazuli and studded with gold stars — was set directly on the layers of ornamentation (Greek crenelations, lozenges, pearls, ribbons, twists, rosettes, scrolls, foliage, diamond-points, stars, denticles, zigzags, chevrons, checkerboards, scallops, ringlets, ovolos, waves, acanthus and olives) that teemed like a tangle of vipers. On the floor, polychromatic mosaics fashioned from glass, marble and lustrous ceramic created a spiral design so vigorous that it provoked nausea and vomiting in Pina if she moved her pregnant body across it too quickly.

There were corbels and cupboards, works of faded passementerie, torn crimson velvet curtains, majolica vases, libraries whose books would fall to dust if their pages were turned too fast, magazines and journals of various periods, sofas of cracked leather that surrendered dust clouds when they were sat on, a canopy bed with sawed-off columns, a television on an empty crate of oranges, closed Venetian blinds screwed tight to the frame whose staved-in slats allowed an opaline light to filter in, contrasting sharply with the furor of the sun outside.

The two men slept in the nook underneath the stairs, by the sundial. On the landing of the stairway, they had set up a kind of mezzanine complete with chairs, a table, a television balancing on the balustrade, rifles and cartridge belts in one cranny and flasks of wine between the balusters. Banners of the national soccer team stretched from one pilaster to the next. That was where the two men drank, smoked, played cards and whiled away their days. They halted all activity and turned off the television when Pina Di Vita, emerging from her oval chamber, appeared at the top of the stairs. They escorted their young charge whenever she set foot outside, their rifles slung over their shoulders, barrels pointing at the earth.

The apartment of the hunchbacked sisters, as inseparable as the two humps of a camel, gave out on the flagstone corridor that ran between the kitchen and the little chapel. The camel sisters were pious, and they knew their way around a stove!

Pina Di Vita, the *sorelle cammelle* and the two men sought the calm life, individualism and complacency among the beams, steel scaffolding, ripped galvanized sheet metal, mounds of plaster and mortar, worm-eaten joists, decapitated columns, cracked tiles, exploded marble, handicapped cherubim, destroyed pediments, broken windows and falling moldings.

They never moved the wheelbarrow full of ruined plaster that was tipped over in front of the door. They never cleared away the beams that had fallen across the staircase. The heap of debris in the dining room remained a heap of debris in the dining room!

They stepped over it, they walked around it, they respected the neglect because it was sacred . . . sacred because it wasn't theirs. To take the initiative and push aside rocks because they kept a door from opening properly was so complicated as to be unthinkable.

No one wanted to emerge from his languor and torpor for a heap of stones. Instead, they slept . . . The women lay down in their beds, in their black under-skirts, and the men snored, head on a table, balancing on a chair, bent over a balustrade or even standing upright, face pressed against the decorative molding.

And how they ate! Three times daily, the humpbacked sisters prepared an enormous steaming cauldron of *pastasciutta* awash in tomatoes, eggplants, ricotta, mozzarella and a sea of olive oil. The household slurped it all down. The noodles slapped against their palates and their lips shone like the halos in a Giotto fresco!

Never was a comment made, a conversation begun or

a polemic launched. They turned the pages of magazines and newspapers because they were there to be turned. They didn't watch television, they contemplated it. The cathode-ray screen shot out a thousand colors, a thousand fires, a thousand movements, a thousand dramas, and that was a lot to assimilate for the residents in their dreamy state of prostration in the midst of these magnificent ruins, sacred and lost in a sea of olive trees. The men watched every soccer match. They simulated pleasure when their team won and emitted the usual complaints when it lost. The *sorelle cammelle,* when they weren't praying in the chapel, missed none of the television dramas imported from Mexico, Argentina, Brazil or America, translated into Italian.

Meanwhile, Pina Di Vita learned the culture of death! Poor girl . . . Bound up in her pain, she would ask, "Where is my lover? Where is Milli?"

"The sea took him . . ."

"America?" she wept.

"Yes, America," the camel sisters answered, their eyes bright.

Order reigned supreme in the house. The apparent disorder hid a harmony of structure: the split flagstones kept the doors from opening, the planks and beams made the staircases dangerous, the squares of marble blocked the entrance, and the tipped-over wheelbarrow was right where it should be. The mountain of stucco sitting in the center of the entryway had become a hieratic object; the men doffed their caps when they passed it and the women crossed themselves!

They stepped around the piles of gravel, using a network of well-traveled footpaths and never disturbing a thing. If, by some false step, they moved a stone from its rightful place, they hurriedly put it back, for that stone was sacred . . . sacred in the sense that it possessed the power to disturb.

Over time, a thick coat of dust had covered everything in the house. The dirt issued from the ceilings, the walls, the floors, everywhere. It transformed the nature of objects and living things: the clothing cut from basic fabrics came to look as though it had been fashioned from the most delicate chiffon. Human faces appeared leaden. When they moved, the residents looked as though they had stepped from Dante's Purgatory. When one of the men slept standing up, his face pushed against a length of marble molding, he resembled nothing more than a grotesque telamon twisted out of its function by Sicilian exuberance and irrationality.

As for the black underskirts, they remained the deepest black.

But, suddenly, the perfect order was disrupted. When the child killed its mother by being born, its little body did not end up in the hole with a Bible and a crucifix. The mother was dead. Nothing remained of her but her blood, and her blood must be allowed to live on, even if it did flow in the veins of a bastard boy. The only person in the world who carried the blood of the late Pina Di Vita could not be put to death. That simply wasn't done.

Signore Di Vita sat on the staircase. Close by him, in a state of collapse on the steps, wrapped in a dark coat, her contorted face hidden behind a veil of black silk, Signora Di Vita wept like a hysterical mourner. She swallowed her tears, which she promptly vomited up, along with foam and bile and blood. She gnawed at the marble edges, she broke her nails on the paneling and wailed inconsolably.

In the chapel, in a state of wonderment, the hump-backed sisters watched over the baby, who was wearing a crown of black flies and lying in a half-barrel stuffed with swaddling blankets. Above, in the oval room, intimidated, the two men walked with heavy tread around the mortal coil of Pina Di Vita. Her skin was turning blue; soon rigor mortis would set in.

Signore Di Vita had cause for concern. *Sangu lava sangu,* he thought; blood cleanses blood. The newborn would live, he knew. He would live, but not on this island. He is as blue as night, as green as the olive, and I fear him . . . At the zenith of his beauty and strength, when his testicles are as big as olives, he will return. He was born on this island and he will return to it. They all return to the womb when vengeance calls. In his veins flows the blood of his murdered parents. I decapitated Milli Palme, his father, and I crushed Pina, his mother. This little bastard will return to stand before me. I can feel fate speaking to me. My destiny is being shaped. It will fall upon me and my prosperity. *Sangu lava sangu* . . .

Signora Di Vita lay on the steps, her toothless mouth full of blood. Signore Di Vita grabbed a rifle and a cartridge belt and strode down the stairs. He went out. He began to walk, trampling the tomatoes drying on the flagstones under the relentless, maddening sun.

"Cursed sun . . . Cursed sun . . . Cursed sun," he shouted, firing a volley of lead in its direction. His lamentation came from afar, from the soul, the earth . . . His cries echoed the cries of Sicily, its tragic history and endless pain. He shouted. He fired. He shouted. He fired. He shouted. He fired. He shouted. He fired . . . When the last cartridge was spent, he collapsed on a sea of tomatoes.

The uproar and rifle shots roused the household. Everyone gathered at the tall gothic window; no one dared step outside. Signore Di Vita's face and shirt were stained red, and they wondered whether tomatoes or blood was the cause. They were afraid. Had Signore Di Vita taken his own life? They feared the damnation of his soul for all eternity. The humpbacked sisters had already begun telling their rosaries, murmuring *Ave Maria*s and

Our Fathers, while the two men stood lifeless, deep in the paralysis that centuries of pessimism had purified.

No one stirred.

In the sky, swallows served notice of their departure for Africa. Meanwhile, on the staircase, Signora Di Pina gave up the ghost.

God, had things gotten complicated!

II

Far away, on a distant continent, a walker out for an evening stroll meditated on these words: "Night isn't black. Night is blue."

Hoping to throw off the sense of despondency that had dogged him for at least the last hour, he stopped in front of a mountain of garbage cans and gutted plastic bags. At first, neither sound nor movement seemed to issue from this great pile of trash. Yet the patient, attentive observer might catch a rustling sound, ever so slight, then growing louder . . . and would realize that there were rats in there as big as housecats!

Rats were rarely seen. A length of scaly tail here, some mangy hide there, a pair of eyes like onyx chips and short, high-pitched cries. The heap of garbage was like a king's ransom, a fetid feast for these rodents whose incisors were yellower than necrosis.

The walker reached into his cashmere coat; the stock, trigger and cylinder of his revolver were wrapped in tulle. The serial number on the barrel had been filed off. He discarded the weapon. It disappeared into the pile of trash as into a surging, dangerous sea. For a moment the rats froze, then came a rustling sound again, then a second, a third . . . Life resumed, as teeming as it was horrifying.

At the end of the street, the sun began its lazy ascent towards the heights. The wind tore away vermilion leaves. They turned circles for a time, then blew down the cracked concrete of the street. It was cold. The sky, gray. Flocks of Canada geese dared to fly above the skyscrapers, en route to the marshlands of the eastern United States. It was autumn again in North America.

Dear and tender reader, the walker meditating on the blue-tinged transparency of the night is none other than our orphan protagonist, our Sicilian bastard. The son of Milli Palme — the bold-hearted poet — and Pina Di Vita — the teenager who called upon *La Madonna* when it was good — *and* of the wrinkled Olive who'd sworn to make war on the Patriarchal Tree.

We know how the Olive was thrust into the young woman. Did the Olive participate in the procreation of the Sicilian child? It certainly did! And if the narrator had not suggested this combination, who would have believed such an allegory possible?

This young man is the son of the Olive, and nothing can change that!

After his life was spared *in extremis,* the Sicilian orphan was given to a family leaving for North America. He crossed the Atlantic with his head buried in the impressive bosom he shared with the legitimate son, since they were twins, to all intents and purposes, for as long as the crossing lasted.

Once he reached America — *Buon' Amèrica* — the Sicilian bastard was entrusted to the Albertini family. The good Albertinis spoiled the newborn for several months before receiving the order to hand the child over to the Donnini family, who delivered him to the Castellanis, who abandoned him to the Boldinis, who expedited him to the Traconellis, who shipped him to the Darellis, who left him with the Baronellis, who pressed him on the Petrillis, who introduced him to the Filippis, who sent him to the Milanis, who handed him over to the Maratonis, who brought him to the Colavitis, who whisked him over to the Di Pontis, who carried him to the Gabrinis, who lent him to the Leopardis, who . . .

Poor little angel!

Every mother cried when the child arrived, and when he departed. These saintly women, plump and bursting with maternal affection, would have sworn before the *Santa Madonna* that this angel-child from Most High was the victim of a villainous plot concocted by some obscure authority whose ubiquity rivaled the Lord Himself's — but trying to save the child would have been unthinkable. As for the men, they accepted the responsibility in silent complicity.

Signore Di Vita feared *Sangu lava sangu* — the fresh blood that cleanses blood spilled. From his very native Sicily, he had stalled the destiny of the little orphan. The exits were walled up, the cracks plastered over and the origins wiped out.

After all, wasn't Signore Di Vita the grandfather?

And he told himself, over and over again, "That bastard had his life spared because of the blood in his veins, and that's enough as it is. Now he lives in an invisible prison . . . Codes and laws are perpetual chains. He is bound in North America like Prometheus to his rock. Both had their chains forged in Sicily. What a mythology! How beautiful it is! Those chains were necessary. I decapitated his father, repudiated his mother, crushed his identity and constructed his prison. At the height of his beauty and strength, when his testicles are as big as olives, he will return. He was born on this island, and he will return. They all return to the womb when vengeance calls them. The Sicilian who has suffered humiliation is as single-minded as a salmon in the month of May: one leaves the vastness of the Atlantic to spawn, the other the vastness of America to strike. But the traces have been scattered. He will drift on a sea of inertia until his dying day. And I can sleep for all eternity with no unpleasant surprises to trouble my rest . . ."

The Sicilian bastard who threw away the revolver knew nothing of that. He had been baptized Olivo Oliva before God. Olivo for his olive-shaped head, and Oliva for his testicles, like a pair of pickled green olives.

The branches of his family tree were as complex as Western democracy. He was condemned to perpetual immobility — *Prometheus Bound* — and at the first false move, he'd take a bullet where it counts . . .

Olivo Oliva lived dangerously, and in his veins flowed the oil of the Olive.

A few days later, it was still autumn in North America. Olivo Oliva, sitting by the tall windows, swallowed the last shapeless ice cubes. Luxury automobiles sped down smooth avenues. The shiny pavement reflected the lights and colors of the city; a rainshower had created that effect. The young man was fascinated by the autumnal play of moving headlights, blinking neon signs and fleeing human shapes trying to get out of the rain. His glass was empty. The restaurant was entombed in the late-afternoon silence that comes after the noontime customers have left and the evening ones have yet to appear. Behind the counter, Cocco, the boss, was scrutinizing his books while the two waiters, at a table in the rear corner, were drinking wine and playing a melancholy game of cards. Everything seemed gray in the restaurant, even the light. Gray light! Imagine it . . .

Olivo Oliva was waiting. The idea of calling for another drink wouldn't have crossed his mind, for fear of disturbing the universe.

"Olivo Oliva!" Cocco called abruptly.

"What is it?"

"Pardon me, I've interrupted your meditation. But Mr. Apandollo just called. He'll be late, an hour or so."

"An hour?"

"That's what he said. I took the liberty of preparing this dish for you. It'll make the time pass faster."

"Thank you, that's very kind."

The two waiters stepped forward and set plates on the table: cheese, dried tomatoes, olives, ham, squid salad dripping olive oil, bread and a bottle of Corvo.

"Would you care for some music? Do you want me to change the lighting?"

"No, thank you, Cocco, no music. Only silence . . .

And don't touch the lights! I love the end of the afternoon at your place. Gray light, everything motionless . . . You can watch the seconds killing the seconds. A wonderfully rare sense of disorientation!"

"You understand! I wanted to create a special atmosphere, something typically Sicilian. What you call a wonderfully rare sense of disorientation, I call the desire for death — that's my restaurant! If you need anything . . ."

"Very kind, Cocco," Olivo Oliva said with a smile.

The *padrone* returned to his books, his accounts paid and unpaid, while the waiters carried on with their melancholy card game. Olivo Oliva ate and drank slowly. He was a young man, thirty years old. He remembered his very first meeting with Mr. Apandollo. His memories flitted by, like in a film: space and time, scenes, settings, protagonists, a plot, breathless zooms. Making movies in his head was his favorite pastime, for he had nothing else to do.

Mr. Apandollo was a short, plump, austere man. He loved gold, and was so irritable that he seemed to be in a constant state of ill humor. He spent an excessive amount of time caring for his neck beard, which he pretentiously called his "Hadrianic beard," in honor of Hadrian, the architect-emperor.

The celebrated first encounter took place in the company warehouse of Apandollo — *Uva da Vino*. Olivo Oliva remembered it well. An imposing spectacle: a glassed-in office atop a network of steel girders, like a lookout tower, amid hundreds of thousands of cases of grapes buzzing with wasps drunk within an inch of their life. Mr. Apandollo was a wine-grape merchant. He liked to tell people he hadn't gotten into the business for the filthy lucre but for reasons of *cultural transcendance* — his words! He'd come to North America alone, his hands jammed into empty pockets, his eyes keen, with a meager list of words he could stammer out besides his arabicized dialect. Young Giuseppe "Joe" Apandollo, having studied the Italian community in North America, concluded that something was missing: a kind of *spiritual tonic*. His words again! All those immigrants traumatized by the crossing and the fresh landscapes ruined their new existence with melancholy memories of the lost homeland. They all lived in a state of inertia, a lethargic reverie, as if the entire community had been struck with malaria. "This disposition of the soul is a cultural manifestation; the soul must be invigorated, its quintessence brought out," thought young Giuseppe "Joe" Apandollo.

Then one day, back when he was apprenticing as a waiter in a restaurant and serving a pair of newlyweds, a magnum of Marsala slipped from his hands. It crashed onto the table and burst. The effect was magnificent. The flowers, silverware, porcelain and the sweets in their little chiffon packets swam in red wine. The table-cloth boasting the colors of Italy was turned into a drooping rag, stained garnet-red and dripping. The poor bride wept like a suffering madonna. Her dress, bulked up with a crinoline petticoat and decorated with silky bouquets, looked like an enormous purple, shriveled grape. Poor thing! Her stunning beauty — for all young brides possess great beauty — had wilted like a flower deprived of water, light and earth.

"Wine! Wine! Wine!" cried Giuseppe "Joe" Apandollo, before falling victim to a storm of insults and blows.

The spilled Marsala inspired in him this idea: the community must have the possibility of making its own wine. Dead origins would be brought to life, and a bridge of culture would span the Atlantic, between America and the Old Country. The idea was revolutionary, when you consider that these Italo–North Americans — most of them former peasants and poverty-stricken craftsmen — considered wine as something reserved for religious services, frozen in old canvases with cracked varnish, ornamenting tables groaning with wealth. The cardinals in Rome drank wine; industrialists from the north did, too. As did the handful of landowners who bled Sicily dry every morning while they ate their *biscotti*. For these peasants and craftsmen — future immigrants, all — whose daily bread was just that, except at Christmas, when they decorated it with a meticulously crushed tomato, wine was something they could never hope to enjoy.

"So many things happen in a glass of wine. Wine gives courage and crystalizes nostalgia. We must make it and its production part of the lives of all Italo–North American families."

That was the revelation young Giuseppe "Joe" Apandollo had as he stood before the Marsala-soaked tablecloth.

Apandollo — *Uva da Vino* bought up the harvests of thousands of acres in California and sold them to the Italian communities along the Great Lakes, on the shores of the majestic Saint Lawrence River and along the East Coast of the United States. The Italo–North Americans bought the grapes, crushed them, fermented the must and created homemade wine, full-bodied, capricious and alive.

Thanks to favorable "arrangements," Giuseppe "Joe" Apandollo earned the tolerance of the Canadian and American governments for his private production. Apandollo — *Uva da Vino* faithfully paid a "commission" on every case of grapes sold. Miraculously, those payments kept troublemakers from cutting in on his monopoly.

Olivo Oliva remembered his very first meeting with

Mr. Apandollo. The warehouse belonging to Apandollo
— *Uva da Vino* was a labyrinth of columns made out of
cases of grapes — cabernet sauvignon, merlot, zinfan-
del, pinot noir, malmsey, alicante, lambrusco, grenache,
barbera, muscat — which attracted wasps, then killed
them. The cases towered to the sky, and oozed. On the
floor, pools of must gathered, speckled with black and
yellow abdomens. Complex networks of runnels
and gutters carried the cadavers towards catch-basins.
The air was heady with wine. Perpetual fermentation
raised pungent vapors that caused momentary intox-
ication. Grape gases refracted the light, and new
combinations of color dazzled the eye.

Olivo Oliva splashed through this swamp of crushed
grapes, damp leaves, shredded stems and sticky juice.
He had to be careful not to slip on loose grapes. The
ground was heaped with insects that buzzed and died
and crackled underfoot.

"I'm going to wreck my new shoes in this damned
lunar landscape . . ."

"A lunar landscape! What a fine image," the young
man thought as he spotted the brightly lit office located
between two columns of muscat. He climbed the iron
staircase and knocked at the door. It opened.

"Mr. Apandollo, I am Olivo Oliva. And your warehouse reminds me of a lunar landscape!"

"What lunar landscape?" retorted the merchant; his

impetuosity was typically Mediterranean. "You've never been to the moon! How can you say this place looks like a lunar landscape? The belly of the Coliseum in Rome, now that would be an image closer to reality. On the moon, there is nothing but death and dust. Here, there's life, culture, poetry. When I contemplate these cases of grapes, I see a lung. It breathes in and breathes out. Its breath is hot. The belly of the Coliseum and my warehouse are two lungs. They breathe the same way, in a single breath, heavy with glorious memory and languid nostalgia. I beg you, young man, come in and close the door. So many wasps! You understand . . . Come in, sit down . . . Let me show you something interesting. Come here, tell me what you see, right there."

"A cage?"

"Very good. Now, what else?"

"A canary."

"Your powers of observation are fair to middling. Open your eyes. Walk around the cage if you need to."

"Okay, I see a cage hanging from the ceiling on a steel wire, a young bird hopping between three perches, a feeder full of seeds, a little fountain with red liquid in it. What is it?"

"Wine."

"You give your canary wine to drink?"

"To keep him singing. The way drunks do. Go ahead, continue."

"A lettuce leaf stuck between two bars, some dropped seeds, a sheet of newspaper on the floor of the cage, covered with droppings. That's all I see."

"That's not bad. Now, sit down, in that chair. Care to drink something?"

"Certainly."

Olivo Oliva sat down. Crossing his legs, he noticed that a muddy paste of flattened grapes and shredded leaves covered his favorite pair of shoes. The mixture featured several dying wasps whose wings still beat like tiny electric motors.

"Young man, there's a washroom behind the door, if you'd care to take a few minutes to clean your shoes."

"No, I'm all right."

"Are you sure?"

"Very sure."

"You have wings on your feet."

"Like Hermes."

"Right, like Hermes. The god of those who search . . ."

Olivo Oliva cast his eyes towards a piece of furniture representing a stuffed rhinoceros. The effect was stranger when Mr. Apandollo lifted a plaque of stiff skin from the animal's flank, for inside it, all decorated with angled mirrors and small red lights, were shelves stocked with bottles and clean glasses.

"Very nice!"

"It's English. Damned blokes." A silence fell. "Your

name is Olivo Oliva, is it not?"

"I am Olivo Oliva."

"And how old are you?"

"Twenty or so."

"And do you know why you're here, Mr. Olivo Oliva?"

"You are a master, and I am a student. I'm here to learn a trade, and you're going to teach me that trade."

"Twenty years old! A fine age to learn a trade. Especially the one I intend to teach you . . . Cinzano?"

"With plenty of ice, thank you."

Mr. Apandollo looked satisfied. Olivo Oliva noticed two photographs above the stuffed animal: Franklin Roosevelt, architect of the New Deal, and a man out for a stroll, wearing a goatee and a Panama hat, in front of the Temple of Concordia in Agrigento, Sicily.

"An English rhinoceros, an American president and a Greek temple in Sicily — what confusion," the young man mused.

"Here you are. With plenty of ice."

"Thank you."

"To your health."

"*Salute*."

"Olivo Oliva, are you sure you don't want to clean your shoes?"

"No, I'm okay, thank you."

"Too bad! Poor shoes. So handsome and so stained.

But very light, I'm sure . . . because of all those wings. Bzzz!" Silence settled in again. "Do you know the name I gave this canary?"

"No."

"Toni."

"Toni? That's a nice name for a canary."

"I thought so too." Another silence. "Tell me, young man, do you think Toni possesses intelligence?"

"Intelligence?"

"Yes. Is he able to form relationships between objects and events? In his brain that's as big as a lentil, do you think there's a shadow of metaphysics?"

"A shadow of metaphysics?"

"Yes, that's what I said."

"I don't know . . ."

"Don't answer with 'I don't know.' I want a yes or a no."

"Yes, there is a shadow of metaphysics in that lentil — I mean, in that brain."

Mr. Apandollo looked doubly satisfied. His fierce eyes shone with fresh light, and he could not sit down, so full of emotion was he. His impeccably tailored suit, however, suffered no agitation whatsoever, and the canary jumped gaily among its three perches.

"Olivo Oliva, Toni is a well-trained bird. I can leave his cage door open, and he will never try to fly away. He might step out just to stretch his wings, but you can be sure he'll go back into his cage once his time is up. You noticed the newspaper at the bottom of the cage. Do you know what that paper is for?"

"To catch the droppings?"

"Exactly. And do you know, when there's no paper at the bottom of his cage, Toni simply doesn't move his bowels?"

"That's impossible!" Olivo Oliva said in wonderment.

"But true! He can maintain his discipline for several days. I don't know where he picked up the habit, but I swear I never taught him that."

"I believe you."

"But the fact remains," said Mr. Apandollo, his voice dropping, "that when there's paper, Toni moves his bowels. When there's no paper, Toni doesn't move his bowels. What do you think about that?"

"I'm astonished!"

"You see, I'm a touchy man . . . Very touchy, even. I've come to see touchiness as a great virtue, a quality. Imagine! I've asked myself this question, and I'd like you to answer it too. We agree that Toni possesses a sense of metaphysics — and that he moves his bowels only when newspaper is covering the bottom of his cage. Fine. Now, tell me, Olivo Oliva, what does Toni think when he sees me spending hours sitting in this chair reading a newspaper?"

Mr. Apandollo had a natural disposition towards splitting a single hair into thousands of strands. A form of delectation that could easily slip into absolutism and madness. Toni deposited a turd bigger than a hazelnut. Quite an effort for a bird whose head was the size of that nut! Outside, thousands of wasps performed a lazy dance by the picture windows, as if the brightly lit office was their womb. The stuffed rhino shot him a wide-eyed look, Olivo Oliva would have sworn to it. This entire miniature world seemed to revolve around the Sicilian's sophistry!

"Do I have to answer?"

"Yes."

"What kind of answer do you want? How am I to know what goes on in that brain that's no bigger than a lentil? There's no logic to it. It's completely foolish."

"Now, now, don't get upset. You are a student. I am the master and I am going to teach you something: in this office, there is a hierarchy. I am at the top of the ladder and you, Olivo Oliva, are at the very bottom. You will not violate this code of respect at any time. Nor will you tell the other person what you think, even if it's 'completely foolish.' Do I make myself clear, young man?"

Mr. Apandollo stepped over to the cage, opened the door and gently picked up the canary. Toni accepted the embrace. Only his head and neck emerged from the man's large hairy hand.

"My resolve is steadfast, and I am awaiting the outcome of your reflection," he said, determination in his face.

He blew on the bird and whistled its song. The canary pecked at the black hairs on his hand, thinking they were thin worms. Did Toni possess a sense of meta-physics or not?

"I can't answer your question. Anyway, I suspect you're just trying to start a quarrel and engage in polemics for their own sake."

"You do please me, Olivo Oliva . . . Long ago, Cicero observed in the nature of Sicilians this enjoyment of controversy and rhetoric. Imagine that! You are criticizing me just as the famous orator criticized my island compatriots, two thousand years ago. Sincerely, young man, you have made me happy."

The happy man picked up a pair of shears and *schlack!* a wing fell like a length of yellow silk floating on a breath of air from nowhere. The bird protested, its left wing beating, a bloody stump of humerus where its right wing once was. *Schlack!* The second wing landed on the floor with its fellow, with equal grace. Mr. Apandollo opened the office door and threw the bird as far as he could, into the forest of cases of wine grapes.

"Too bad, he sang so beautifully," he said, soaping his hands. "Your intervention could have saved Toni."

"Intervention? What intervention?"

"I warned you, I'm very touchy. You could have curbed my sensitivity. You chose not to. In my way of seeing things, this bird was plotting. Don't you understand that? Toni moved his bowels on a newspaper I spent hours reading. I see conspiracy and impudence in that attitude! I'm sure of it! You could have demonstrated the contrary. You did not stay my hand, nor did you soothe my spirits."

"That bird was plotting against you? He was mocking you?" Olivo Oliva burst out, stunned by such enormous nonsense.

"I specified that it was 'in my way of seeing things,' and in that area, all rights are mine. If I decide the earth is flat, then it's flat . . . and I'll get along quite well with that new arrangement. I am lord and master of my psychology because, as a Sicilian, I've never been lord and master of my island and its history. Such sad revenge! I am Sicily on two legs, even if I live in North America. When I move, I am the crystalization of more than two thousand, five hundred years of disconsolate occupation. When I walk, all the sorrow of Sicily walks with resignation. When I escaped to North America, I thought I'd be able to deconstruct and remake my identity anew. Alas, I fell into a much crueler trap: nostalgia as hard as concrete. My emotions no longer come from the heart; they issue from my head. I have lost all passion; now, I am just haughtily preoccupied. What you call vanity, I call vertigo. What you consider complacency is my quest for perfection. Obsessive apprehension governs all my violent acts . . . Mr. Olivo Oliva, if I tell you that Toni was plotting against me, you can be sure he was."

Mr. Apandollo picked up the two wings.

"Look. The triangular wing is like the shape of Sicily, and this other one, spread out, looks like North America . . . But something is missing. Once we had a bird that sang and beat its wings. Now we're left with two inert limbs and the memory of what united them. That's nostalgia: to possess two dead wings and remember their movement and music . . ."

Mr. Apandollo snapped open his handkerchief and carefully wrapped up the pair of wings.

"Here, this is for you. It might not have much meaning today, but tomorrow . . . in a few years . . . I'm sure it will. This folded handkerchief contains Toni's song. A wing for Sicily, a wing for North America, and nothing in between to make them fly. With the years, the labor will be devastating. And it will take you God knows where . . ."

Olivo Oliva extended his hand to take the handkerchief. When Mr. Apandollo calculated that he had the best possible angle, he delivered a blow so hard and fast that the young man's head almost flew from his shoulders.

"Olivo Oliva, stop looking at me that way. And while you're at it, unclench your teeth, they're going to pop out of your mouth. Not one word from you! No questions either! I am the master and you are the student. The handkerchief is on the floor. Pick it up. I'll get you another glass, yours fell under the table. I wanted this moment to be engraved in your memory forever. And now, it is. You'll never forget the slap. And you'll never forget Toni the canary's song. What a slap it was! Your head almost flew off. Pick up the handkerchief, it's a precious object now. An entire world is contained within it."

Olivo Oliva slipped the precious object into the inside pocket of his coat and began contemplating the photo of Roosevelt. Mr. Apandollo turned around slowly. He would have to live with the silence and stillness of the cage. He had sacrificed his little yellow animal for the sake of an emblematic demonstration. Already, the death of Toni the canary weighed heavy on his soul.

Outside the office, behind the cases of cabernet sauvignon, a cloud of wasps was busy working the bird's remains. Its eyes were gone and its tongue had been devoured, down to the first vertebra. Farewell, Toni.

For several minutes now, Cocco had been trying to shake the young man out of his reverie.

"Olivo Oliva," Cocco called loudly.

"Farewell, Toni . . ."

"Mr. Oliva!" Cocco called again.

"What? What's going on? What's wrong?"

"Pardon me, I'm interrupting your thoughts again. I am terribly sorry. Mr. Apandollo called. The second time! He wants you to be patient for another hour. Can I offer you something? I see the bottle is empty."

"Farewell, Toni . . ."

"Excuse me?" Cocco said.

"Toni was devoured by wasps. He didn't even have his wings to fly away. An angel without wings, in hell . . . Imagine!"

"Who's Toni?"

"Am I still sitting by the tall windows?"

"You haven't moved. Nothing's moved here. As a matter of fact, nothing's moved for decades."

"You're right. Nothing has moved. Cars go speeding down the smooth pavement. The wet street reflects all the luminous frenzy of the city. People out walking flee the downpour."

"Olivo Oliva," Cocco interrupted, "do I bring the other bottle or not?"

"Why not?"

"Fine, I'll be right back."

"Thank you, Cocco . . . and farewell, Toni."

"Toni! Who is this Toni?"

Olivo Oliva watched the waiters. As one pondered his next move, the other slept with his head thrown back, mouth open, his cards deployed like a fan. Hesitation hovered in that decerebrating inertia, in the gray luminosity where seconds killed seconds.

"Here's the bottle. What are you going to do now?" Cocco asked.

"Drink it and wait for Mr. Apandollo."

"If you need anything . . ."

"Thank you, Cocco."

The young man took a healthy swallow of wine, then returned to his memories of another time.

"With a slap like that, how could I have forgotten Toni's song? Poor Toni!" he thought. And he rubbed his cheek, the one that had been punished by the blow.

Scenes flowed through his memory, following his fancy. Mr. Apandollo was late, the bottle was full, its contents were good, and Olivo Oliva had nothing else to do.

"What a slap! My hand has gone completely numb!" Mr. Apandollo exclaimed.

"I'm sorry for you."

"Here, drink this. Cognac from France. It might relax the convulsions that are currently deforming your face. So young and so disfigured, what a shame! All that for a slap! And all that hatred inside you . . . I can feel it, it's grotesque. Hatred is a bottomless pit! You slip over the edge, you fall, you're intoxicated by the sweet excess free of all reference, and emptiness brushes past your face. A lyrical decline that leads straight to death. Not biological death, but death as a metaphor . . . You must never surrender to hatred, especially for the person you wish to harm. Hatred is a passion! And a being devoured by passion turns disorderly, and in turn creates disorder around him! Olivo Oliva, you're here to learn a trade, which means learning order. Besides, hatred disturbs your grooming! To strike properly and cleanly, your hair must be well groomed. That will spare you messes of all kinds . . . What are you looking at?"

"Roosevelt."

"Roosevelt!"

"Yes. Isn't that Roosevelt there on the wall, above the rhinoceros? What a strange photo, all yellowed and wrinkled and torn. It looks like it traveled around the world in someone's old suitcase."

From his chair, Olivo Oliva contemplated the photo. Standing, Mr. Apandollo did the same. They drank in silence and considered the portrait of the American president, as if they were meditating.

This was the first moment of complicity between master and student. There would be others, of course, but none as deep as this one.

"Strange," Mr. Apandollo commented, "that picture has been on the wall for years, and this is the first time I've seen it. I mean, really seen it. God, how old it is . . . You see, Roosevelt is my companion. I crossed the Atlantic with that photo. It's the only thing I brought from Sicily. What a story — a half century ago! That picture used to be pinned to the wall of the house where I was born. A one-room house, and that room was our bedroom, dining room, kitchen, shed, workshop and stable. Suffocatingly hot in summer. During the winter, we would warm ourselves by the fireplace, and the big mule would be our radiator at night. Chickens and piglets would scurry between our legs. There were no windows; daylight came through the open door. We all slept in the same big bed: my father, my mother, my grandmother, my brothers and sisters. From above our heads, Roosevelt and the Madonna watched over our sleep. I remember it very well. The poverty! All adversity came from Rome, that decadent, lazy whore laughing and frittering away our labor. The city where sadistic princes and haughty bishops kiss each other's hands. The capital of a shiny but impotent bureau-cracy, malevolent, incapable of understanding Sicilian reality. Rome bled us dry with taxes and dispatched her army when our bellies cried out too loud. And then that cursed capital massacred the sons of Sicily; it sent battalions of young men, too young to have started shaving, off to wars that didn't concern them, to coun-tries whose names they couldn't even pronounce . . .

"As poverty ground away at us, America became our imaginary capital, Roosevelt our mythical president. Almost every Sicilian had a Roosevelt pinned to the wall — never a Mussolini, a Cavour, a Garibaldi or a Pope . . . Roosevelt and the Madonna, Amen. In that cursed land, we dreamed of America. The America of myths. Monolithic America. The America of wide-open spaces, big cars speeding down endless highways. The America of graceful women with long legs, long legs that went on forever . . . America with no limits, optimistic, good, generous, just and industrious. Frank Capra's America!"

A brief silence fell.

"I left Sicily when I was fourteen. What a story! Listen to this! In class, the teacher, who was a fresh convert to the Black Shirts, spat in my face every time I made a mistake. My father was a Communist. Six mistakes added up to six gobs of spit and a storm of insults. Think about it! In school, in the street, in the fields and even in the little house where I was born, there was constant humiliation — impossible to lift up your head. My eyes never rose from shoe level. One day, I stopped looking at the image of the Madonna and I lifted my eyes to Roosevelt. My life changed. I went from sordid inertia to feverish action. One day, before I went off to school, I carefully removed Roosevelt's photo and put it in my pocket. In class, I pretended I didn't understand something the fascist teacher said. I went up to him and hit him in the face with a sickle. My classmates fell into a stupor of admiration. What an image! I'll never forget it! Standing at the front, completely at a loss, I stared at my friends and called out to them, 'Do we agree with this?' And in one voice they answered, 'We all agree!' Meanwhile, the teacher was lying across the desk, bathing in a pool of blood. Half the sickle was sticking out of one ear. The blood turning black before my eyes — that's what was most frightening! Then I turned and went back to my desk."

"Excellent revenge!"

"Olivo Oliva, you didn't understand a thing. You've got it all mixed up. In the springtime you do your planting, and summer is the time for rest. In the autumn you harvest and in the winter you prune. That was no revenge; it was an act that had to be carried out in a particular order. Black shirt, insult, gobs of spit and sickle. Planting, growth, harvest and pruning. Nothing more, nothing less."

"If you say so . . . Didn't you get arrested?"

"Of course not! You understand, from his ancestors the Sicilian has inherited poor eyesight. Often he is mute and very nearly deaf . . . and it's all relative. I was deathly afraid. Everything went spinning around my desk, around my head, as if every object traveled in a heliocentric orbit, and I were the sun . . . the sun of the classroom. I gave off an energy that made objects revolve and dance in their orbits until their motion made me nauseated. It was my first homicide, you understand . . . the nausea, the culture shock! My friends went on working with their faces in their books and papers. They lifted their eyes when the Angelus sounded and pretended not to notice that the teacher had a sickle stuck in the middle of his face. As simple as that! What audacity! Suddenly, the classroom was lousy with carabinieri. But they couldn't make those little devils spill the beans. They hadn't seen anything, they hadn't heard anything . . . 'All of you had your noses in your books and you never noticed that your teacher was being murdered?' the Prefect shouted. And do you know what those little Garibaldis replied?"

"No idea," said Olivo Oliva, enjoying the story.

"It was magnificent! Gabrielli, who shared a desk

with me, to cover for me stood up and said in the most natural voice possible, 'When I'm working in class, nothing can distract me. I want to be one of the carabinieri too, like you gentlemen. And to do that, you have to be very, very intelligent, isn't that right? I'm very sorry, but I still have a long way to go.' Then big Peppino chimed in, 'All the time I've been a student, I've gotten slapped because I never worked in class, and for once I apply myself, and the police criticize me. Mr. Prefect, sir, you have to decide what Italy wants because, frankly, I just don't know any more.'

"Every student added an attack against the police, against the State, against Rome. It was wonderful! Delicious! Meanwhile, my face was as white as paper and my smock was covered in vomit, which irritated the carabinieri even more.

"Believe it or not, the Prefect had to call off the investigation: there was no proof, no motive, no clues, no leads, no evidence . . . No nothing! A fine tale, wouldn't you say? Those schoolboys all protecting me with their youth and effrontery. I left my village the very same day. The sea took me and I reached America in classic style, with two hands in two empty pockets and a picture of Roosevelt in the third. And I never saw Sicily again!"

"Your eyes are red . . ."

"My eyes are always red."

"Is Sicily still as poor?"

"Who can tell? You should know, I send a lot of money back to Sicily. All my old schoolmates receive an annual payment. They deserve it. Thanks to them and their impertinence, I'm here, a rich man. I also help my aged mother and my brothers and sisters. They all live in new houses and drive Alfa Romeos, they eat meat and drink wine. I've been able to lift my family and my village out of their eternal poverty. A lot of Italo–North Americans do the same. By sending our dollars to Sicily, we're raising the place out of its Third World stagnation, something that Rome could never do! And that explains my friend Roosevelt."

Mr. Apandollo took out another handkerchief and patted away the tears that glistened in his Hadrianic beard.

"Why the Doric temple?" Olivo Oliva asked softly.

"What Doric temple?"

"There, in the second photo, there's a Doric temple. The Temple of Concordia in Agrigento."

"Do you know that temple?"

"I've seen it before in books about architecture and art history. It was built some 450 years before Jesus Christ, six columns across, thirteen deep. It was turned into a Christian church in the sixth century, and that's why it's still standing. At twilight, the stone absorbs the slanting rays of the sun, and at those times, the temple appears in all its splendor, as golden as olive oil."

"A temple as golden as olive oil?" Mr. Apandollo cried.

"What's the matter, what did I say?"

"Olive oil?"

"Yes! Olive oil."

"Olive oil!"

"Olive oil."

"Olive oil . . ."

"Yes, olive oil. What's going on?" the young man asked.

Mr. Apandollo went over to the picture, filled with an anger that seemed to come from nowhere.

"What about him? Do you know this man who's standing in front of your olive oil temple?"

"No."

"Olivo Oliva, you were supposed to look at the man before you looked at the temple! The temple comes from somewhere else, it's Greek. It was erected in Sicily by Greek invaders. But this man, he's Sicily's greatest son! Don't you know him?"

"No."

"A shame."

"If you say so."

"You want to learn to kill, and you don't know this man?"

"The trade was forced on me. The trade came to me."

"Keep quiet. And get this into your head: this man's name is solitude. Sicilian solitude. The solitude of the hired gun, the *sicario*. To become yourself, completely, you must travel into solitude. You must be alone . . . the place of finding yourself. Oh, Pirandello, forgive the ignorance of this apprentice *sicario*!"

There was a violent pounding at the door. Olivo Oliva wheeled around, afraid. Five men came in. Their appearance was comical, but something about them suggested it was better not to laugh. They were dressed in black suits, they wore gloves, and they were armed with .12-gauge shotguns. Their faces were hidden under sheer white masks held in place by velvet two-cornered hats decorated with red plumes and embroidered with a thousand gilded baubles. These figures were the plenipotentiary emissaries of powers and interests that appear on no map!

"Perfect . . . The initiation can begin," decided Mr. Apandollo, the *Maestro sicario*.

"What initiation?"

"Yours."

"Mine!"

"Of course. You are about to embrace a new life, and the change must be sanctified. Initiation possesses the prodigious ability to transform a man into something else. That way, you will be closer to God."

"They say that initiations are traumatizing or painful — sometimes both!"

"They work better that way."

"Do I really have to go through it?"

"Good Lord, do you ever ask questions! Without this ordeal, you will be nothing more than a common criminal. Homicide is punishable by universal legislation, and that's the way it should be. As *sicarii*, disorder and the non-observance of civic organization are our antagonists; tranquillity and order are our allies. With this rite, you will become a unique individual with the privilege and right before God to take life. Homicide, through this initiation, will become an act both sublime and absolute. Without this ceremony, you would remain a small-time killer, and I have no interest in that race. The Ministry of Justice might wish to study them, but me? Never! The *sicario* is no barbarian, because of his sense of the sacred."

Olivo Oliva said nothing.

"Never forget that the *sicario* practices the world's oldest profession. The popular adage maintains that prostitution is the oldest profession — so be it! Take shelter behind that convention that brings a smile to everyone's face. Blend into the popular consensus. You will possess that skill, because the *sicario* is like the chameleon: green on a green leaf, gray on gray stone, but never outside its nature as a chameleon.

"Contract killing is the oldest profession the world knows. It dates back to the birth of Man somewhere in Africa. With the first palisades came the first communities, the first psychologies and the first behaviors, the first ideas and the first cultures, the first policies and the first religions, the first polemics and the first undesirables. Contract killing is, and will always be, a political and cultural act. Without those aspects, the *sicario* would not exist. There would be only common criminals!

"Man, the olive tree and the hired killer's profession all have their origins in Africa. All three spread northward at different eras; they crossed the Mediterranean and struck Sicily, which became their place of predilection!"

A moment's hesitation.

"God in heaven, Olivo Oliva! When I tell you these things, I suddenly realize why Sicily is so violent. *Mamma mia,* could it be true?" cried Mr. Apandollo, *Maestro sicario*, astonished by his own discovery.

The initiation was a true ordeal. A preparation of boiling olive oil was applied to the apprentice *sicario*'s right hand. The hand swelled up immediately, shedding strips of fried epidermis, along with a fingernail or two. Then the hand was thrust into cool olive oil. That process relieved the burning, kept the eruption of blisters to a minimum and sped the regeneration of damaged tissues.

This rite of initiation — purification of the hand by boiling oil and inoculation of the initiate with the *sicario* strain by application of cool oil — has its origins somewhere in Africa. It moved into the Mediterranean through primitive Asia, then Egypt at the time of the XIXth dynasty, and next the Greek islands — and finally, like an act of blind destiny, it struck Sicily.

Today, could we state with certainty that Sicily has a supernatural propensity for cultivating the olive and for cultivating death? Mr. Apandollo meditated on just that issue.

Olivo Oliva moaned in pain. A stream of snot connected his nose to his necktie. His eyes turned back in his head, his face was wrought with convulsions, and he was drooling. His right hand marinated in a silver pan in which, by a strange mystery, golden olive oil transmitted through punished flesh and burst veins the solitude of the *sicario*.

The *Maestro sicario* had just discovered something. He was thinking out loud. His student heard nothing. Before him stood the five men, like so many telamons lending pomp to this odd liturgy. To the right of the fifth ambassador, in the cage hanging from the wire, a lemon now took the place of Toni the canary.

That was a lot for a first meeting inside the lungs of Apandollo — *Uva da Vino*.

"Where the hell did that lemon come from?" the young *sicario* wondered out loud, and then fainted.

Once more, Cocco attempted to shake Olivo Oliva from his reverie.

"Olivo Oliva," he called out.

"What? What is it?"

"Dreaming, as usual . . . Mr. Apandollo just called again."

"Again? That's the third time. It's not like him."

"The third time it was! And it is strange. Anyway, he won't be able to have dinner with you this evening. He wants you to be here, tomorrow, at the same time."

"Do I have a choice?"

"Not really."

"So I'll be here tomorrow, at the same time. Now what do I do?"

"You want something to eat?"

"Yes, I'm still hungry. What's cooking in your kitchen?"

"Anything you like."

"Ravioli, maybe? I'd take a mountain of ravioli!"

"Very good. I'll go see the chef and tell him — "

"Cocco, wait, there's no hurry! I'd like to ask you something. Do you have a minute?"

"Of course."

"Here, sit down, let's have a glass of wine," said Olivo Oliva, grabbing a clean glass from a neighboring table.

"*Salute.*"

"*Salute.*"

"You see, Cocco, you're the kind of person who

has an idea about everything. People even say you have caustic opinions about the sun. I'd like to have your point of view on a certain subject . . . an abstract subject."

"Go on."

"Here it is: it has to do with replacing a canary with a lemon."

"What?"

"Replacing a canary with a lemon."

"When you say 'canary,' are you talking about the bird?" Cocco asked.

"And when I say 'lemon,' I'm talking about the fruit," Olivo Oliva added happily.

"It is original."

"I'll explain it to you, Cocco. The bird lives in a cage. It dies and it's replaced with a lemon. Surely you must have an idea about that."

"Uhh . . . is the lemon yellow?"

"Yellow like a canary."

"Is the canary yellow?"

"Yellow like a lemon."

"A yellow lemon takes the place of a yellow canary, is that it?"

"That's it."

"You want my point of view on that?"

"An idea, a reflection, an image . . ."

"The visual effect is striking! A three-dimensional

optical illusion." Cocco hesitated. "Replacing a yellow canary with a yellow lemon is . . . it's like throwing a stick in place of a boomerang — that's my idea!" Cocco cried abruptly, his arms crossed, his head held high.

"Bravo! It's wonderfully absurd! It's like saying: Why is there something instead of nothing? You throw a stick, and you're caught in a wild spiral between nothing and something. The world can turn upside down because the stick falls here, instead of there. Cocco, you're something else!"

Olivo Oliva gulped down his wine. He seemed filled with sweet euphoria. Cocco didn't care for that. He was calculating all the angles. There was way too much nonsense in the formulation. All that abstraction had him worried. He wanted to plane it down, cut it back, standardize it. The boss turned towards the table where the waiters were playing.

"Oh, Domm!"

"What?" Domm called back impatiently.

"Forget about your cards for a second. Listen to this riddle, I just invented it: What do you call a boomerang that doesn't come back?"

"A stick."

"You knew it?"

"Knew what? I have peasant roots and all I know is simplicity. And a boomerang that doesn't come back, in my village, where I'm from, we call that a stick. And you break my concentration for that! People are disturbing me on account of Australian folklore! *Madonna santa!*"

Domm threw his cards on the table, grabbed the bottle and poured the contents into his sleeping friend's open mouth.

"Hey, Giovan . . . Wake up. The boss wants to hear riddles."

Giovan drank. The wine bubbled against the sides of the bottle. At the last bubble he opened his eyes, got to his feet and went over to his boss without so much as a stagger.

"I'm talking to you, Mr. Cocco, you who offered me this black-market job in this most beautiful restaurant, in this enormous country. And why not you too, Mr. Olivo Oliva! Listen to these subtle riddles. I thought them up, at night, all alone in my bed, thinking about the Old Country. Here's the first one: What was the greatest universal cultural catastrophe?"

Silence answered him.

"You give up? The burning of the library at Alexandria."

"Bravo!" cried Domm.

"And now, good sirs, watch out for this one. It's more delicate, and so sensual. Who is the most beautiful woman, clothed or undressed?"

"I don't get it," said Cocco.

"Come on, boss! You own this so very pretty restaurant, and you pay so few taxes. This riddle was specially designed for your refined cerebellum. Unless I'm mistaken, of course. Listen carefully: Who is the most beautiful woman, clothed or undressed?"

"That's just erotic poetry!" Cocco protested.

"The odor of femininity makes my blood run hot," Olivo Oliva whispered.

"The Italian woman from Montreal," Giovan declared proudly, strutting like a peacock.

Domm clapped his hands. He was obviously very pleased with how things were turning out.

"Mr. Cocco, let's spice up the sauce a little, what do you say? Pay attention to this one, she is as tough as nails. If you find the solution, I will work in your restaurant for a year, and you won't pay me a penny. But if you say uncle, you'll give me a raise."

"If I get it, you work for free. And if I lose, I raise your pay," Cocco repeated. "I accept!"

"*Madonna!* I couldn't take it any more. Thank you, boss, the riddle was burning up my tongue. Be careful, now, here it comes: What does the aristocrat keep, the worker spit and the poor man swallow?"

Cocco thought hard. He took a few sips and turned to Olivo Oliva.

"What do you think?"

"That the riddle comes from Sicily, and that I'm in North America."

The restaurateur pondered it for several endless minutes. Silence took hold of the room again. Seconds were killing seconds . . . And the gray light was as gray as ever! Cocco drank wine. Olivo Oliva drank wine. Domm and Giovan too. They all drank wine and waited for something to happen. An action, no matter how minuscule it might be. And not necessarily the solution to the riddle!

"Uncle!" Cocco cried out.

"Are you sure, boss?"

"Uncle, and you can have your raise."

"So, good sirs! What does the aristocrat keep, the worker spit and the poor man swallow? *Snot,*" Giovan declared proudly.

"Snot!" Olivo Oliva burst out.

"Snot. That's good, very good," Cocco said calmly.

"Now, boss, I'll give you the chance to win it back. I have one last riddle. This time, I don't want anything, I don't want to abuse your generosity. If you answer correctly, Domm and I will work, not one, but two years for not a penny. Imagine the savings!"

"And if I don't answer correctly?"

"I want nothing for myself. But you give him a raise."

"You give me a raise," Domm added.

"I accept."

"Bravo, Mr. Cocco! You are a true prince! What bravado! Now, watch out, here comes the riddle: Why did the sister of the Count of Cavour take swimming lessons?"

"The Count of Cavour! The architect of Italian unification!" exclaimed Olivo Oliva.

"No! The Count of Cavour, the architect of Sicilian misery," Cocco replied sharply.

"Excuse me, sirs, but this is no time to be talking politics. Two raises are at stake here. The moment is critical! So, Mr. Cocco, do you want me to repeat it?"

"No, that's all right, I understood. Let me think . . . Oh, hell, I give up. Uncle!"

"And you give Domm a raise in pay."

"I give Domm a raise in pay."

"Thanks, boss."

"You, Mr. Olivo Oliva, do you have any thoughts about this riddle and its solution?"

"I don't know enough about the history of Italian unification. I didn't even know the Count of Cavour had a sister."

"*Madonna!* Who's talking Italian unification? Mr. Olivo Oliva, I'm the one telling the riddles here. I'm the artist and that gives me the right to arrange all the realities the way I want to. If I decide that the Count of Cavour has a sister, well, then, he has a sister. And if that sister looks exactly like a she-ass, well, then, she *is* a she-ass."

"She is a she-ass," Domm declared.

"A complete she-ass," Cocco certified.

"Now, let's get serious again," Giovan broke in. "Mr. Cocco has cried uncle. Domm can count on his raise. And our friend Olivo Oliva knows nothing about the glorious history of the glorious unification of glorious Italy. Perfect, everything is as it should be! My dear friends and Italo–North American compatriots, do you know why the sister of the Count of Cavour took swimming lessons? To work as a whore in Venice!"

"To work as a whore in Venice," Domm declared.

At thirty years old, Olivo Oliva was a *sicario*. A famous contract killer. Every year, he committed eight or so murders in exchange for shoeboxes full of dollars. He hadn't really chosen the profession. It had been thrust upon him. We know that much. But he turned out to be an honor to the trade.

Taking a life wasn't a complicated business. Mr. Apandollo and Olivo Oliva would get together for a friendly glass of wine. *So many things happen in a glass of wine . . .* They would murmur sibylline sentences. The young *sicario* would receive the order and a few recommendations.

"You should build a dome," said the master.

A dome, in their language, designated the person to be slain. To build a dome was code for "to construct an architecture above his head," in other words, to carry out exhaustive research to select the time and place when the condemned man was most vulnerable.

"But don't build it too high," Mr. Apandollo went on. "You don't have much time, and the pipistrelles might get in your face once you hit the rafters. Those little bats aren't so blind, and they hear everything, and fly while you sleep. Don't go too deep, either, the foundations are shaky, the cement is watery, and the bricks are like calves' liver."

"I'll go in minimal," the young man concluded.

"That's it, be minimal, but not modern."

Olivo Oliva was good at his job. He performed it the way a mason accomplishes his, with the generosity of the craftsman who loves and has mastered his trade.

The great stonemasons had erected cathedrals. The *sicario* brought down the domes . . .

"I brought down the dome," he would report.

"May God protect the architecture," Mr. Apandollo answered calmly every time a dome fell.

The domes had to fall according to a very complex code of professional ethics, a set of rituals several thousands of years old.

"It's the delicate little touches that separate the *sicario* from the common criminal," Mr. Apandollo liked to say.

The *sicario* must always approach the dome face to face. They both belonged to secret hierarchies, and this was a sign of recognition and great respect.

The *sicario* must always smile before pulling the trigger. That was important. "Though I stand before you, armed," that smile signified, "please understand that it is not a personal initiative. You know that. We could have shared a glass of wine together. But life has decided otherwise! Today, you are considered undesirable, but I am not here to judge you. I know that once you were an open and curious child, fascinated by a procession of ants, concerned with a fledgling that had fallen from its nest. I, too, was once that child. We could have put that fledgling back in its nest together. Where were you? And where was I? Now you are here. And I am here, too. Our friendship will have lasted a second. It will have existed. I shall keep this second like a precious gift. Farewell, friend."

Then the *sicario* would pull the trigger! A bullet. A single one. There. In the heart, never elsewhere. The *mamma* would have the pleasure of scratching out her eyes and weeping a river of tears over the perfect face of her revolverized son. Good night, little angel returned to God on High.

Olivo Oliva had no trouble killing. The domes that were to fall with a tug of his finger were not really human beings. Actually, they were, but they belonged to a different world. A world that had no affinity with what we know and experience daily: universal suffrage, art and culture, politics, the Holy Roman Apostolic Church and taxes. These men and women (a woman could be a dome, it was rare, but possible — Olivo Oliva had never known one personally) lived elsewhere, illicitly.

In our democracy, in precarious harmony, a great number of secret lodges and parallel societies coexist. Their branches are like the tributaries of the Amazon that flow into other tributaries of the Amazon, that flow into still other tributaries . . . These organizations have their codes and laws, an economic system, a foreign policy with heads of state, ministers, banks, weaponry, agreements and a culture: that of the hedonism of death till death itself. These second-category societies flourish by fastening themselves faultlessly onto first-category ones, like blood-sucking lampreys on the bellies of magnificent fish. Or, better still, like those rat communities that teem in urban basements. We never see them, but we know they're there, well adapted and well structured. Rodents need human society to live and proliferate. Whether society needs its rats is another issue.

The young *sicario* brought down his domes in underground stealth. He dug down, smiled, aimed for the heart, fired . . . and returned to the surface. Then he went quietly out to eat, alone with his newspaper.

Olivo Oliva was untouchable, inaccessible to the illicit hierarchies because he remained on their periphery, and unsuspected by official justice because he had no official existence. The young *sicario* traveled between two worlds, with no sense of belonging. In North America, no one could say who he was.

Olivo Oliva owned a collection of passports, birth certificates, social insurance and social security numbers, citizenship documents, credit cards, library cards, driver's licences, and they were all false, under false names, continually renewed for security reasons. Even his membership card at the Worldwide Badminton Club on Baker Street in London featured a false name: Gordon Zola.

In North America, no one could have imagined where he came from. Not even him. Several families had taken in the infant, for it was their destiny, shedding silent tears all the while. But all that had happened long, long ago. Those vicissitudes had helped develop a garland of polymorphous personalities in the young assassin's mind. "I am a collection of tiles from a ravaged mosaic, thrown to the winds," was his favorite saying.

He suffered from his affliction. Would he ever succeed in reconstructing the wreckage of his identity and build an image of himself? But how can you build a self-image when the image, as image, does not exist? How could he be Olivo Oliva, knowing that Olivo Oliva did not exist? The poor young man, ensnared in allegory and imagination to keep from being swept away by murderous melancholy, drifted on a sea of inertia, here in America.

Meanwhile, in Sicily, Signore Di Vita feared *sangu lava sangu*.

What if Olivo Oliva was Olivo Oliva the way an actor is? An actor, a real one, is someone who plays a role with all the desired psychological complexity. The work is difficult. The better he portrays that psychology, the warmer the applause. After the performance, he takes a shower to cleanse himself of the residue of the stage, and goes out for dinner with the rest of the company. He's famished. He gave his all under the lights.

Sitting at the restaurant with the men and women of his profession, the actor calls for ravioli. No one can change his mind; he makes the same request night after night. The entire crew knows that when he asks for ravioli, he wants the kind stuffed with ricotta and spinach, and not the other kind, with meat. The actors all know each other. The atmosphere is happy and uproarious. And their happiness has nothing to do with the crowd and the greasepaint!

From the very first mouthful, the actor leaves his character and slips deliciously back into real life. It is a very special moment, like the last shaft of sunlight disappearing into the sea. The very last shaft. Where you can see the color green, the green of the chromatic spectrum. You have to be very watchful, because it lasts only a second or two. To see a green sun at the far reaches of the sea is a spectacle of strange beauty that can burden the soul with sadness. And to see a magnificent protagonist eating ravioli and returning to the state of an ordinary taxpayer is just as awe-inspiring!

On stage, on the other hand, we never know what the ravioli are stuffed with. Who can say? Stage ravioli have not been lovingly rolled and stuffed by a cook. Sent up from the basement where the property shop is, they are a metaphor that helps express the play. Therein lies the splendor of the theater: the harder the stage ravioli strive to be authentic, the harder the audience claps its hands. The stage is an outsized perversion that plays with life the way a cat toys with a mouse. A place where art, with its faculty for the abstract, imparts an appearance of gastronomy to inedible plastic ravioli.

Which is why our actor sitting down at the table, surrounded by his comrades, eats heartily, whereas he never touches his plate on stage. He knows intuitively — the stage being the place where intuition must arise — how fragile the theater is, and that it can collapse under a mound of real ravioli stuffed with ricotta and starred with shredded spinach.

So who is Olivo Oliva? An actor? Olivo Oliva is much more than an actor. With his mouth full of ravioli, he is a dream streaking towards the real, with no idea that paying your taxes is also part of real life.

"How can I be Olivo Oliva when I know I'm not Olivo Oliva? With the help of art," the *sicario* concluded.

Olivo Oliva was an artist. He had his own museum, which he called "The Imaginary Museum." A closed room whose air was so rich in thallophytic vegetation that it irritated the bronchial tubes. The place was heaped with bizarre objects atrophying in inglorious darkness.

There was a zebra skin nailed to one wall. It was so faded that the black stripes had disappeared. Next to it, on a shelf, stood a dozen bronze Remington sculptures, cowboys and Apaches. A glass-and-oak case contained a collection of fountain pens: gold, silver, steel, ivory, mother-of-pearl, metal, plastic, wood, aluminum, marble and glass. They were polished, separated, shaded, branched, plated, watered, mixed, striped, spotted, marbled, embroidered, inlaid, speckled, chromed, mottled, dotted, engraved, inset, incrusted, gilded, in colors of burnt Sienna, mud brown, lily white, emerald, black, mahogany, poppy, lilac, jonquil, chocolate, cream, coffee, tobacco, claret, bottle-green, gooseberry, dove-white, turquoise, earth-tone, mouse-gray, ruby, brick-red, cobalt blue, coral, salmon, aquamarine, azure, auburn, saffron yellow, hazelnut, ultramarine, sepia, opaline, rust, ebony, amber, violet, carmine, indigo, copper, orange, tawny, purple, the reds of Persia, China and Venice, the blue of Prussia and the green of Veronese, peach, cherry, plum, olive, blood-black, canary and lemon. Next to the display was a headless Saint Michael the Archangel, ceramic dragons spitting red and blue flame, blocks of marble, a photo of Benito Mussolini with his fingers in his nose, cases of Marsala wine, a majestic, semi-spherical stone that, when set on a *trapetum*, was used to crush olives for oil, a bilingual French-English dictionary, a red marble Madonna, the bust of a Roman general, a Norwegian flag, two silk-screens signed by Therese Nortvedt, a shattered mosaic and much, much more . . .

And it was all engulfed in dust. God, was there dust! The collector had to live with it and admit he was also collecting dust.

"I'm collecting dust, too," Olivo Oliva said every time his nose reddened. And the dust made him sneeze!

This assortment of curiosities revolved around a central object: the very lovely *Greek Slave-Girl* by the English sculptor Hiram Powers. Arranged as the centerpiece of his Imaginary Museum under a miserable electric lightbulb hanging on a wire, this statue, sculpted out of veinless Carrara, shone among the hodgepodge of objects and styles like a goddess in her temple.

The *Greek Slave-Girl* was exactly as she sounded. In a pose both vulnerable and haughty, she awaited her fate in a slave market. Her head was modestly turned to the left, as if avoiding the malevolent eyes of potential buyers. Her hair was bound in a chignon, according to the Hellenic style, but her profile was Florentine with a nose that dropped straight down like a cliff. A dimple split her chin, an attractive trait in her case. The *Greek Slave-Girl* had beautiful shoulders, nymph-like arms, and her buttocks were shaped like mandolins. Her breasts formed two domes that owed more to an architectonic idea of rotundity than to the sensual curves of a real woman. They seemed abnormally far apart, an effect created by the dusky nipples. And the veil of dust that covered the young prisoner only served to heighten the human drama of her situation!

The *Greek Slave-Girl* wore handcuffs on her wrists. Her chains were the symbol of her condition. They underscored her distress and synthesized the obsessive, degenerate representation of a kind of eroticism that took its full measure of morbidity when you realized — quickly enough — that the English sculptor dreamed of being in the market for slaves himself.

That was true enough. Hiram Powers, a mediocre imitator of the Italian style, spent his life sculpting, fabricating — from the world's best-quality marble — saccharine copies of Greek slave-girls. Damned bloke!

Such was the Imaginary Museum. Every piece in the collection had been altered by a layer of dust. Every piece . . . except for those celebrated breasts. They shone under that stupid lightbulb like the finest silver struck by a heavenly ray of light. The effect was positively mythic. You might think they'd been buffed with a certain amount of devotion. Not at all! They'd just been caressed daily by the museum owner. And had we been able to approach that Greek slave-girl, and smell her stone nipples, and taste them with the tip of our tongue, we would have identified the familiar scent of olive oil!

Olivo Oliva was an artist. A painter. In between contract killings and a sea of inertia, he painted canvases as vast as North American space.

The painter's first encounter with the conceptual, pragmatic world of modern art is a story in itself. The face-to-face initiation took place during a school trip to his city's Fine Arts Museum. At the time, Olivo Oliva was just a schoolboy. His pretty teacher was enamored of contemporary art. She organized the visit in order to introduce her students to modernity. What an idea! The exhibition — "The Dialectical Surface in North American Painting" — created in her a sensation of intense well-being. Ecstasy, in other words. She flitted from room to room, as if she were skipping through a flowery meadow on a fine July afternoon, caring nothing for the giggling class that followed behind in a disorderly stream. They pushed and pulled at each other, they grabbed and shoved, they punched each other as they passed the "garbage" that represented the cutting edge of the present age. Even the girls, who were usually very attentive during field trips, were at their most detestable. They screamed, scratched and deposited chewing gum in each other's hair. Modern art had a bad influence on the pupils. The canvases, with their unreadable forms and outlandish proportions, irritated them so much that they flew into a mood of runaway misanthropy. So young, and so misanthropic!

Half blinded by an elbow to the face, Olivo Oliva noticed, in one corner, an immense rectangular canvas, painted blue, split by a vertical yellow stripe, slightly off-center. He moved closer. He was lost in attentive contemplation of its vast surface when suddenly he felt sperm running down his leg. It was the first time, and it was good! This ineffable state of excitement had transfigured him.

Touched and moved, the schoolboy went back to the fray. He swore to return the next day to challenge the mystery of this new pleasure. For a boy in the midst of puberty, it was fantastic! No use of the hands, no references or erotic imagery were necessary. All he had to do was stand before the big painting and stare at blue gushing over yellow. The effect was sensational! Fabulous!

"The Dialectical Surface in North American Painting" lasted three months — from the fifteenth of September to the fifteenth of December — and every day, after school, the warm, streaming semen flowed faithfully with an assiduity that fascinated the young hedonist. A deep and complete surrender filled him each time. When the show ended, the work of Barnett Newman was returned to its Dutch owner and Olivo Oliva experienced his first heartbreak.

The painter-assassin lived in a large studio. One part was for living, the other for painting. The Imaginary Museum was at the rear, to the left.

With two great lengths of steel tubing fastened to the floor and screwed to the ceiling beams, he built an easel that, when two horizontal lengths of pipe were adjusted, would support canvases of all dimensions.

Olivo Oliva always worked the same way. His habits never varied. On the surface of the canvas, he would apply a thick layer of sickening, toxic, corrosive, yellow paint. Next he would mix solvents, rust-proofing and mineral pigments that produced the kinds of yellows he was avidly searching for: from a leaden shade of orange to burnt Sienna, through sulphur, saffron and gilt.

The fumes made his head spin. His breath stank of

turpentine. Nausea wrenched his gut. The canvas became a kind of organic anguish whose pain was so intense it would have brought a smile to Edvard Munch's face. The opacity and heaviness of the form, the storms of oily spots, the nervous eruptions and pools of blood, the strata of color, the slashes and brushstrokes, the clouds heavy with sighs from beyond the grave, the light of dying day caught in this hopeless crisscross of lines — all that would have made the Norwegian master smile!

Near the easel stood a wobbly armchair. Once the work was done and the effect achieved, Olivo Oliva took a seat to rest and even sleep. His hands hung down on either side. They were coated with paint and dripping pigment. They looked like two big, tousled brushes.

When he awoke, the artist would paint a round shape, black and perfectly centered. And that was all!

"One more work of art in the Western world," he would say as he cleaned up the studio.

Olivo Oliva always painted the same object. Once the surface was completely dry, he hung the canvases wherever he could, pushing others aside. They were everywhere: on the walls, in the corners and angles, even on the ceiling. Hundreds of them! A collection of exactly two hundred and thirty-seven paintings of all sizes: little square ones the size of a handerkerchief, and others, immense, rectangular, like entrances to a tunnel. Every one featured that mysterious round, black icon right in the middle.

Round? Not exactly. The more you looked, the more you'd be tempted to call it an ellipse . . . an oval . . . an olive-shaped figure. Yes, an olive!

Olivo Oliva was painting black olives!

But they weren't exactly black, either. Black, but not truly black. Black is the physical meeting of all colors. Olivo Oliva was painting something else, it was his secret. A shadowy business that had nothing to do with what we usually see as black.

Was it that celebrated, penetrating black that stupefies the eye and casts it into the most delectable excess? No. That black is found in Sicily, and we're here, in North America.

This black was dreadful. As frightening as a thousand nightmares contained in a single night. Endlessly fascinating! Were you to stare at it, even for a moment, you would fall victim to somber exaltation, a disorderly obnubilation that leads the eye into the realm of the intolerable. Olivo Oliva took precautions. He believed that if he extended his hand towards that black, it would tear his arm off and shred it with all the violence of an airplane propeller.

Olivo Oliva painted black olives. A black almost as grave and triumphant as the black underskirts of Sicily.

The artist had no idea where his imagery came from.

What was the source of this unhealthy luminosity? What was behind these *olivoid* shapes? How had he been able to compose a shade of black that tormented the eye? Why this extravagant, ever-increasing number of canvases? What inspired him to paint, what pushed him to create works that resembled overripe olives in a grove?

One thing was certain. With single-minded perseverance, Olivo Oliva was convinced of his own genius. He was vexed at having to exhibit his paintings in his own house, instead of seeing them circulate in the great museums of the world's great capitals.

But Olivo Oliva was first and foremost a contract killer. And such a man has no right to a public existence. So why did he do what he did?

"Olivo Oliva, why go to all that trouble?"

"Because it's that way."

"And why is it that way?"

"I don't know."

"Where does it all come from?"

"I think it comes from here."

"What's this?"

"Take it."

"A box!"

"Open it."

"Jewelry."

"A charm bracelet. With nine charms. A long chain with a *Trinacria*."

"A what?"

"A *Trinacria.*"

"What's that?"

"The arms of Sicily: the head of a winged woman, with a serpent's tangle for a headdress, surrounded by three running legs bent at the knee."

"With red eyes?"

"Eyes sculpted from living coral."

"Gold, too?"

"Twenty carats."

"What's that strange smell?"

"It comes from the jewelry."

"The jewelry? Gold can't be altered by any known substance. And neither can it take on an odor, good or bad."

"Yet it's true. Here, smell it."

"You're right. That's incredible! It really smells bad. Gold that stinks — now, that's something new. Can I smell it again?"

"By all means."

"Gold that stinks! Where does that smell come from?"

"I have a theory. But let's hear what you think first."

"If you ask me, it smells like . . . I don't know. A farm, a barn, stables, a sheepfold . . ."

"You disappoint me. You said it yourself: 'Gold can't be altered by any known substance.' Yet this gold is impregnated with a smell. We are in the presence of an extraordinary phenomenon, and the odor must have the same origins — that is, extraordinary!"

"If you ask me, the odor is extraordinarily bad."

"Of course it is!"

"So you're right. And if you're right, it's because you've thought it over."

"This jewelry has gone everywhere with me. I don't know where it's from or how it came into my life. But there it is, and it stinks. That odor haunts me. It gave birth to me, and it keeps me alive. You know I've been driven from pillar to post for as long as I can remember. I don't know where I came from. That smell is a sign. Intuitively, I know it's the smell of my ancestors. If I discover where it comes from, I'll discover my true origins."

"What is the smell?"

"Human misery mixed with olive oil."

"Human misery and olive oil! That's the perfume of your origins? Your ancestors' smell?"

"You said it."

"Do you have any clues, any leads?"

"Everything is contained there."

"The charms and the tri . . ."

"The *Trinacria*."

"Right, the *Trinacria*. The charms and the *Trinacria*. Can I have a look?"

"Of course."

"That's strange — it's beautiful, yet it stinks. Tell me how."

"How what?"

"How these golden, magnificently worked little objects could lead you to a spot that smells of human misery and olive oil. Where your origins lie."

"Your glass is empty. Would you take more wine?"

"Gladly."

"Here's my reasoning. You'll see, it's simple, but it's not simple. Examine these charms. There's a hand. A Doric column. An eye. A stiletto. A sun. A replica of Sicily. A tree. Then there's these two others I haven't identified yet: this oval one that looks like an egg, and this other one, like a tiny spear-tip. This is the *Trinacria*, the symbol of historical Sicily. I'm sure that when they're joined together, these objects will yield a meaning, a mystery. They have to be read like chapters. The chapters have to be put into the right order, as if they made up a book."

"That sounds like literature!"

"What else should it be?"

"That's exciting. Have you started to read, and compose?"

"Not really. Everything is still so vague. The only thing I know is that Sicily shows up twice: the *Trinacria* and this replica with the inset diamond. The diamond probably indicates an exact geographical spot — but where? Then there are the two charms I haven't been able to identify."

"So obscure, and so intriguing."

"Listen, Poloni, the bottle is empty, I'm going to open another one. In the meantime, have a good look at the charms. You never know, maybe you'll be able to figure out the story behind all that stinking gold."

"But it's your story!"

"I'm giving it to you."

"If you insist. And I will look at these charms of yours. Whew! What a smell!"

"I'll be right back."

"Take your time."

A few minutes later.

"Marsala. That's all I drink. Consider the coincidence: it's a Sicilian wine."

"Red Marsala. And your nose is red, too. Another coincidence!"

"It's because of the dust. I have a dust collection in my Imaginary Museum."

"Good for you!"

"So, did you discover anything?"

"Maybe. You say you've never been able to identify these two charms?"

"Right."

"And this tree?"

"What about the tree?"

"Do you know this tree?"

"No."

"For the love of God, Olivo Oliva, fill up my glass, I think I'm about to compose a chapter!"

"A chapter? Tell me!"

"I know this tree. It's an olive tree."

"Are you sure?"

"I am! This twisted trunk, these crooked roots and these few stunted branches. An olive tree! Look at the charm: a sun with rays like daggers. Only the olive tree can thrive under Sicily's murderous sun."

"Now we're getting somewhere!"

"That's not all. The tree is old. Very old. It's a patriarch."

"How can you tell?"

"The history of the patriarchal tree is involved with this thing . . ."

"The *Trinacria*?"

"Yes. The *Trinacria* is the symbol of historical Sicily. I know something about the island's past. Sicily, never the master of her destiny, caught in the vicissitudes of history. The patriarchal olive tree belongs to her: it has known all her invaders!"

"Aren't you going a little too fast?"

"You're the one who told me to write the chapters. That's what I'm doing! Anyway, with an allegory like this one, is there any limit to literature?"

"I don't know. Maybe you're right."

"Besides, I've identified the last two charms."

"Tell me."

"The one that looks like the tip of a spear is nothing more than the lanceolate leaf of the olive tree. And the oval one is its fruit, the olive."

"Bravo! You certainly have a knack for literary fantasy."

"How I detest your arrogance!" A brief silence fell. "Olivo Oliva, your life is unique and captivating. And I'm your friend. The stink that rises off this gold is completely real. The odor is proof that there's no room for whimsy here. So I began to compose. These jewels smell extraordinarily foul. I'm only trying to formulate an extraordinary explanation for this extraordinary phenomenon. Anyway, you're the one who sent me down this path!"

"I'm sorry, I'm a little . . ."

"Most of all, you're worried . . . and damned touchy, too."

"Touchiness is a virtue."

"I've heard that somewhere before. And it always struck me as a cliché!"

A longer silence this time.

"Poloni, I'm sorry. Do you want to look at these charms some more? Do you want a little more wine? Do you want — "

"Listen, Olivo Oliva, I know all about you. I mean,

I know what everyone else knows, which is not very much. You're in search of your identity. Your origins have become an obsession. The more time goes by, the more your quest becomes a crusade. Well, let me tell you that the secret lies in Sicily, with a patriarchal olive tree."

"Impossible!"

"You want literary fantasy? Listen to this, because it's your story. You don't speak Italian; you speak a kind of arabicized dialect found only in Sicily. You have two olives where your testicles should be — you said so yourself! You smell of oil and you sweat an oil-like substance when you play badminton. Your head is olive-shaped. Your hair is naturally oily. Your skin is swarthy like an olive at harvest time. A mixture of oil and blood flows in your veins. And though you don't know it — because I'm sure you don't — you spend your time painting olives!"

"I'm painting olives?"

"You certainly are. You're painting olives — look at all these canvases!

"I hadn't seen it that way."

"That's what I thought. And to take it one step further, you've arranged these hundreds of olives as if . . . how can I put it? As if we were in a grove, surrounded by trees!"

"An olive grove?"

"An olive grove. Even your name refers to the olive."

"Go on, go on."

"There's nothing more to add, except that the whole business begins back there, in Sicily. You're probably right, as you said yourself: the diamond set into the replica of the island points to a particular place. Perhaps you'll find the patriarchal tree there. As for the other charms, I have no idea of their meaning. The hand, the Doric column, the eye, the stiletto — what do you think?"

"I think we'll have to keep writing chapters."

"Let's start with chapter one! The eye, for example, is synonymous with vengeance."

"The stiletto signifies 'to strike in darkness.'"

"The hand means 'to give succor.'"

"The Doric column stands for Western art."

"Olivo Oliva, I believe that vengeance is calling you back to Sicily."

"What for?"

"To save Western art."

The two young men broke into noisy laughter.

"How strange it is! Listen to this, old friend. There are three main elements: the olive — and you're one yourself — Sicily and a patriarchal tree. The way I see it, you need to return there to find that olive tree. You have a mission, and it can't be denied. Once you get there, I'm sure the other chapters will open up before you — like a book! But only once you're there. If you're called upon to avenge something, then you'll do so. But now, it's obvious, you have to leave, put North America behind you and fly above the Atlantic, back to the Mediterranean. You are an olive in search of a patriarchal tree in Sicily. Now, that's a novel — a beautiful novel! It's all so beautiful!"

"Come on, Poloni, there are billions of olive trees in Sicily! How am I supposed to find the right one? And you know very well I can't leave town without Mr. Apandollo's permission. He'll never let me go. Not even for a beautiful story." A brief silence fell. "How long am I supposed to go for, anyway?"

"A day, a decade, a lifetime . . . Who can say? Gold that stinks — now, that's extraordinary, and that extraordinary stink is summoning you back to Sicily! The first thing is to go back to that island. And then . . . "

"Then what?"

"Then the beauty of literature . . . Everything will open up before you. The charms will reveal more secrets. And you'll discover what there is to discover. Nothing more, nothing less. But if you do nothing, with the passage of time, North America will become a stagnant cesspool rotten with sadness, nostalgia, immobility, apprehension, aborted desire and, worst of all, you'll go on painting black olives that sicken the viewer and building that olive grove with its chaotic perspective. I'm sorry, Olivo Oliva, but you have no choice!"

"But you know what I do for a living! You know Mr. Apandollo!"

"I know your profession. And I know Mr. Apandollo. Believe me, he's aware of your condition. He doesn't want you to live in the same distress he does, the same melancholy leading to death. Mr. Apandollo is a sensitive, generous man, and he knows how to listen. Besides, he loves you like a son. Tell him about the gold that stinks, the patriarchal tree and Sicily. He'll understand and give you good advice. I'm sure of it. Didn't you have supper with him this evening, at Cocco's?"

"No, he canceled. He put it off till tomorrow night."

"Tomorrow night, at Cocco's? That's the perfect time, the perfect place! Olivo Oliva, you simply know too much now. It'll become infernal. If you do nothing, your life will be hell forever. You have to act, and now's the time. Tomorrow night, talk to Mr. Apandollo. He'll help you."

"You really think so?"

"Don't underestimate him. More things happen inside his head than in all the glasses of wine in the world. Olivo Oliva, the future belongs to you. You must attack it head on." A silence fell. "It's nearly two in the

morning now, and I'm sleepy. This story, this wine . . .
I'm going home, it's late."

"Poloni, wait, I've got a riddle for you."

"Go ahead."

"Do you know why the Count of Cavour's sister took
swimming lessons?"

"To work as a whore in Venice."

"You knew the answer!"

"I made it up in the first place."

"Oh!"

The next day, it was still autumn in North America.
Olivo Oliva was waiting by the tall windows. That was
his spot. Mr. Apandollo was late again. The ice cubes
were melting in Olivo Oliva's glass. They were about
to disappear. Shiny luxury cars sped down smooth
avenues. The glistening pavement reflected all the colors
of the city, and we know where that effect comes from.

The restaurant was entombed in silence. The same
silence as the evening before. The same as last week, last
month. A silence imported from Sicily, two thousand,
five hundred years old.

Cocco frowned as he examined his open books. The
two waiters, their raises in their pockets, played cards
with fresh sadness. Olivo Oliva spotted a majestic

formation of Canada geese flying between the skyscrapers. The birds slipped behind a tower of glass, then reappeared, farther on, before disappearing again. They had left the taiga of Quebec, near James Bay, for the sunny climes of the American Southeast. But who cared about that?

The ice cubes had melted. Strips of lemon peel swam in the water. The migrating birds were far away. The young killer thought, "It's Wednesday. The geese must have left James Bay yesterday, at first light. They'll follow the Appalachians and Friday, they'll be wading in some warm marsh in Delaware, or North Carolina, or even South Carolina, or maybe even Georgia. Four days to cross North America, from top to bottom. What an adventure!"

"Excuse me, Olivo Oliva . . ."

"What is it, Cocco?"

"Another one?"

"Another what?"

"Mr. Apandollo just called."

"And he'll be late?"

"He'll be late."

"An hour?"

"I don't know. He wants you to sit tight and be patient. Do you want anything? Something to eat, something to drink?"

"I'll take another one with lots of ice."

"Very good."

Giovan was sleeping with his head thrown back, his mouth open and his arms hanging. He looked like a revolverized body, mortally wounded, right there, through the heart. Domm was still hesitating over his hand. That card, or this one? Or maybe the other one?

Cocco returned with a drink: a lot of vermouth and a lot of ice happily singing against the glass. He put it down and went back to his figures. He, too, seemed irritated by Mr. Apandollo's delay. Who knows, maybe Cocco had something to whisper in the *Maestro sicario*'s ear?

Olivo Oliva spotted a second group of palmipeds flying south. They were too far away, he couldn't identify them. He recognized the V-formation, that was all. Where exactly were they going?

The young *sicario* took a few sips. His eyes had shifted downward, slipping slowly, very slowly, the way a shadow obeys the declining sun. Olivo Oliva looked at his cashmere coat thrown across a chair, to his right. The inside pocket contained the fateful box.

He gave a smile of satisfaction. His life had reached a new summit, and the birds migrating south were nothing compared to what was about to occur . . .

Olivo Oliva took the box from his pocket and placed it on the table. With great care, he lifted the cover. The glittering, stinking gold. He had nothing else to do. He was passing the time. The seconds had to be killed. He untangled the charm bracelet. He freed one of the *Trinacria*'s feet, which had gotten caught in a link of chain. He counted the fluting of the Doric column. He ran a length of chain between his fingers. He divided the charms into two groups and compared those that had unveiled their secret with those that had chosen to remain silent.

The odor of the jewelry made his nostrils flare.

"I am an olive in search of a patriarchal tree in Sicily," he said, closing the cover.

The stink had grown intolerable. He slipped the box into the inside pocket of his coat, then turned absent-mindedly back to the tall windows and busy streets. The night was there. Blue. You couldn't see the Canada geese between the skyscrapers, it was too blue out.

The stink of the jewelry hung in the air like smoke. Domm and Giovan emerged from their reverie. They cast sidelong glances left and right. Their memory had identified that acrid scent: olive oil mixed with Sicilian poverty, the earth, the sea, that damned sun . . . Shaken by the odor of the island, the waiters were filled with a burning desire for nothing at all, and for everything at once. They fought for breath. They had spent years burying their memories in dust and death, and now they flared up like fire spat from the mouth of the earth.

Warm, fat tears streamed down their cheeks and wet their white collars, top-quality cotton yokes that throttled their necks.

"Life is falling forward forever, and it hurts," Domm sobbed.

"And wine has us hovering between life and death," Giovan added, lifting his glass.

Then it was Cocco's turn to catch the scent of Sicily. What a commotion! His nose sniffed everywhere at once as he sought out the triangular island inside the walls of his restaurant.

Olivo Oliva saw none of that. Three fire trucks, their sirens screaming out the apocalypse, rushed past the tall windows. What about that young woman, climbing into a taxi? God, was she beautiful! And well dressed, too. He noted the classic cut, the discreet shades and the high quality of the fabric.

He knew her. He'd crossed paths with her one afternoon on the Avenue of the Americas, facing the Future Hotel. The woman had stepped on his foot. She'd turned around, wanting to beg pardon. Her red lips were about to form the words — but no one was there. Olivo Oliva was standing directly in front of her, but she didn't see him. There was a scent she couldn't quite recognize; in North America, people cook with butter. Olivo Oliva was invisible. He was green, a green chameleon on a green leaf. The young woman was perplexed, she was sure she'd stepped on someone's foot. Then she went on her way, her slender heels striking the pavement as he watched her *with eyes that undress a woman.*

Olivo Oliva recalled the episode as the taxi sped off with its passenger, tires squealing. He smiled. He drank and let an ice cube melt in his mouth. He kicked his left shoe off with his right toe and began moving his big toe painfully, the one that had received the blow from a high-heeled shoe as sharp as an awl.

Wrapped in lemony cologne, Mr. Apandollo made a discreet entrance. Every head turned in his direction — every one but the young *sicario*'s. A fourth red truck shot by like a meteor, following the others. Cocco dropped his fountain pen on his books and went to greet Mr. Apandollo. They shook hands warmly and spoke in low tones. Domm and Giovan stood by stiffly in an imitation of Prussian cavalry. The *Maestro sicario* removed his coat and Cocco hung it up for him. They talked at length; first the one man, very meticulous in the presentation of his request, then the other, very attentive and concerned, with a sympathetic ear. Then they shook hands a second time, with few words and sober smiles and old-fashioned solemnity — for an agreement had just been struck.

Mr. Apandollo noted the strange odor that hung in

the air. He climbed the three steps that separated the lobby from the dining room and approached the two waiters, who were still standing. The *Maestro sicario* affected the ostentatious attitude of the man who has just bestowed a favor, and Cocco followed, displaying all the humility of the one who has received it.

"Giovan, how goes it?"

"Very well, thank you."

"And the family?"

"I just had a letter from Sicily. The family is fine, Mr. Apandollo, and I thank you."

"And you, Domm?"

"Very well, and my family, too. Thank you, Mr. Apandollo. Did you know that Giovan and I got a raise?"

Mr. Apandollo turned to Cocco.

"You raised their salary?"

"I had to . . ."

"Giovan and Domm are the best waiters in North America, and they've deserved a raise for as long as I can remember!"

He turned to them.

"Bravo, I'm very happy for you both. Sincerely. If it was up to me, you'd be paid as much as a surgeon, and not a penny less. But what can you do . . . To each his territory, to each his task. Tell me something, friends, did you notice a certain smell? It's hanging in the air like a cloud. Strange, but I feel I know that odor. You wouldn't be cooking up something new in your kitchen, would you, Cocco?"

"No. It started a few minutes ago. Where it comes from, this smell, I can't tell you. But what it is . . ."

"And what is it?"

"It is the perfume of Sicily," Cocco said vehemently.

"My Sicily," Domm chimed in.

"No, mine," Giovan insisted.

"Come to think of it, it's the perfume of my Sicily, too. A mixture of olive oil and human blood," said Mr. Apandollo, *Maestro sicario*, very moved.

"If you'll allow, Mr. Apandollo," Giovan put in, "I'd say it's a mixture of olive oil and sulphur."

"Sulphur!" Domm interrupted. "It takes a son of a sulphurer to come up with something like that. Unfortunately, it's not that at all. True, it is the smell of olive oil, mixed with a very particular odor: that of the earth."

"The earth? Absolutely not!" Cocco exclaimed. "You're completely wrong. You're a son of the soil, nostalgic for your long-lost fields. There is the scent of olive oil, I'll give you that much. But take my word for it, the other smell is that of the sea."

"Nonsense," said one.

"Ridiculous," said the other.

The polemic raged hot. Each man was proud of his

reasoning and shocked by the poverty of the others' arguments.

The fisherman's son swore it was a composition of olive oil and the scent of algae, and eviscerated fish drying in the sun, and *mattanza* on a bloody, foaming sea. The peasant's son maintained that behind the scent of olives were the odors of freshly turned earth, labor under a hellish sun, and animals, outbuildings and the promiscuity of the *latifundium*. The miner's son spoke of the sulphur pits and sulphur vapors, the dank galleries, sweat, and the blind horses that were born in the mine and spent their lives pulling loads without ever glimpsing the sun.

The storm of words was enough to set your head spinning. Mr. Apandollo said nothing because he knew more than the others. He spotted Olivo Oliva watching him, and went to his side, abandoning the noisy gathering.

"*Ciao*, Olivo Oliva! How are you keeping? I'm sorry about last night. I disturbed you for nothing, and tonight I'm late."

"It makes no difference."

"Have you been following the discussion?"

"A bit. A bad smell made of olive oil . . . Those three could call a colloquium for a drop of spilled wine."

"Maybe, but they're right about one thing: the scent of Sicily. Each man has his own Sicily, so it seems . . . But it's still Sicily, just the same. And all polemics are legitimate when it comes to that subject. Maybe you have your own ideas about it?"

"I'm famished," Olivo Oliva replied.

"Me too."

Olivo Oliva seemed ill at ease. Mr. Apandollo noticed and called out to the three men, "Friends, if you please, we're dying of hunger. I beg you, stop your quarreling. And Cocco, for the love of God on High, a bottle of Corvo, and make it snappy!"

Cocco came back with a bottle and two glasses. Domm and Giovan kept on debating.

"Haven't they gotten to the bottom of it yet? Cocco, tell them to quiet down so we can eat in peace."

"Tell them to quiet down? Impossible! They're burning like Vesuvius. So, what can I bring you?"

"The usual. Dried tomatoes, mushrooms San Maurini style, pasta alla Norma, roast veal in virgin oil, braised fennel and cheese."

"Bravo! Now that's an appetite! What about you, Olivo Oliva?"

"Baked olives, snails in oil, ravioli, leg of lamb Agrigento style, artichokes alla Caponata and a half dozen cannoli."

"Bravo! Now that's another good appetite!" Cocco said, pouring the wine.

Mr. Apandollo and Olivo Oliva sat in silence a moment.

"The dome?" the *Maestro sicario* said gently.

"As usual. It fell without a sound," said his pupil.

"May God protect the architecture . . ."

A second silence settled in. The waiters began criss-crossing feverishly, bringing the first dishes: bread, oven-baked olives, snails swimming in oil, tomatoes steeped in oil, mushrooms braised in oil, a flask of oil and a second bottle of Corvo.

"*Buon appetito!*" Domm and Giovan said with their best smiles.

Then they joined the boss behind the counter. All three had the firm intention of picking up the debate where they'd left off.

"So, Olivo Oliva, you don't like your profession any more?" asked the *Maestro sicario*.

"What makes you say that?"

"About the dome, you answered, 'As usual, it fell.' That's the first time I've heard you say 'As usual.' I don't like that word. It's cowardly."

"Really?"

Cocco, Domm and Giovan had resumed their argument. Passion coursed through their veins. They believed they were experiencing moments of great intensity.

"They're at it again."

"So it seems."

"You didn't answer my question."

"Which one?"

"Whether you had an opinion about this miraculous olive oil smell that seems to have everybody excited."

"No. Not really."

The silence lasted longer this time.

"Listen, Olivo Oliva, we've just sat down at the table, and already I have a premonition that the evening will be as tiresome as a monk's cell. You're like a son to me . . . I can feel you're nervous. You *are* nervous. You have something to tell me. So stop trying to hide and tell me what's on your chest. That way, at least, we can have a pleasant meal."

"I know where the smell comes from."

"See, things are starting to fall into place. We're going to have an exciting night!"

"Do you want to see something?"

"Of course."

Olivo Oliva gave the box to the *Maestro sicario*.

"What is it?"

"You can open it."

"Jewelry? And what a stink! What's behind all this?"

Olivo Oliva was tortured by hesitation. He took a great swallow of wine and started talking. And talking. He was like a Tibetan prayer wheel. He spun out his tale: his mysterious origins, his marginal profession, his panoply of false identities behind which was no real identity, the solitude of the *sicario*, the inability to truly live a true life, how he came into ownership of the jewels, how gold could capture this whiff of human misery, the reason for the smell of olive oil, the charm bracelet heavy with symbols, his collection of two hundred and thirty-seven canvases, the patriarchal tree somewhere in Sicily under a murderous sun, the whole allegory, the summons, his desire to leave and, as icing on the cake, those two olives where his testicles should be.

He dug into his wallet and produced a folded hand-kerchief, which he placed in front of Mr. Apandollo.

"Here, this is yours. You remember? It contains Toni's wings. I'm giving them back to you. 'One wing for Sicily, the other for America, and nothing in between except nostalgia — the obsession of a lifetime.' Those were your very words, such a long time ago . . . And what about Toni? Poor Toni, devoured by wasps. Fare-well, Toni . . . Toni never plotted against anyone. Poor little bird, he couldn't have. One wing for Sicily, the other for America, and nothing in between to make them fly. You were right: the work was devastating."

The table fell silent. They had already consumed the entrées, the pasta dishes, the contents of the bread-basket, the flask of oil and the two bottles of wine.

Mr. Apandollo had listened in silence, his eyes traveling from the box to the handkerchief, from the handkerchief to the box. One gave off a penetrating stench, and the other held two dead wings.

Domm and Giovan cleared away the oily plates stained with tomato, herbs and Parmesan cheese stuck to the porcelain. They returned with dishes stacked with meat and vegetables, a second flask of oil and two more bottles of wine. The service was carried out promptly, with an economy of motion.

Olivo Oliva poured himself a healthy serving of wine and fell upon his lamb as though he hadn't eaten for days.

"What do you intend to do?"

"I'll go to Sicily and find that olive tree."

"Then what?"

"Then I don't know! The rest will be my story."

"It's crazy."

"What's so crazy? Here we are, debating the aroma of olive oil and human misery! The aroma of olive oil and the scent of Sicily. To each his own Sicily! To each his own misery! Everything is permitted! This stench is my own. It's calling me and I'm following."

"You'll need a new passport to get out of the country."

"I'm counting on you."

"What makes you think I'll help?"

"Mr. Apandollo, I suspect you know a lot about me. Something tells me you might know everything. I'm not asking for the truth. I'll find it myself, all by myself. I'm just asking you to help me leave. The rest is my business!"

"What do you want me to do?"

"I want to go in peace. I want to be left in peace. And I want to sleep in peace, too."

"Which means?"

"I'm through with the contract killing business. And I don't want any surprises, good or bad. I don't like surprises. You understand what I'm saying?"

"That's impossible. You belong to an order. The slightest defection and you'll have the Most Holy Lodge on your trail. Besides, why would I help you?"

"You're the only person on the planet who can do anything for me. The only one. And deep down, you don't want my false life to be like yours. I know that much!"

"It's impossible," Mr. Apandollo replied after a long silence.

"Why?"

"Olivo Oliva, I don't think you grasp just how serious your request is. You work for — no, you're part of — a very sophisticated, highly organized structure. The slightest anomaly is immediately noticed. Your departure would be too obvious. You'd be tracked down right away. You know what they're like. They're everywhere, they're efficient, and they're pitiless."

"I'm an olive in search of a patriarchal tree in Sicily. With or without your support, I'm leaving. I'm asking you one more time, Mr. Apandollo, to help me."

A long silence.

"I *can* help you." He paused. "Olivo Oliva, let me tell you something. I might look surprised, but I'm not. I've feared this conversation for years. I know your story down to the smallest detail. I know everything about you. The patriarchal olive tree in Sicily is not a false lead. You're on the right track! But I can't say anything more. I swore on my honor, and honor is all that separates me from mediocrity. Breaking that oath would expel me from the magnificent company of *sicarii* and make me a common criminal! Which would mean the fires of hell for all eternity. I'm sorry, I can't say anything more. I gave my word. And I'm a good Christian. But I've thought about all this, and there might be a solution, just one . . . The main problem is how to send you to Sicily without raising suspicions."

"Without raising suspicions?"

"If, for example, the Most Holy Lodge itself sent you to Sicily."

"I don't get it."

"I'll explain. It's obvious that you can't leave on your own. That would never work. I know that much. Sooner or later, the Most Holy Lodge will get its hands on you, and you'll end up sleeping with the fishes. So you have to leave with its consent and even its protection."

"The Lodge is going to send me to Sicily?"

"The Most Holy Lodge, *Sacro Colonnato—Santo*

Consiglio–Regno Dei Cieli,[*] Mr. Olivo Oliva. Always show respect towards the Most Holy Lodge — never familiarity!"

"The Most Holy Lodge, *Sacro Colonnato–Santo Consiglio–Regno Dei Cieli* is going to send me to Sicily! Is that better?"

"That's better."

"Thank you."

"So, you have to leave not only with the consent, but with the protection of the Most Holy Lodge."

"How will I do that?"

"Olivo Oliva, there's only one way for you to leave North America. I've thought it over, and, unfortunately, this is it. Listen carefully. I am a Very Honorable Member of the Very Honorable and Holy Lodge, and you are my most faithful servant. We are protected. If ever a misfortune befell us, if ever we were in danger, we would immediately be covered. This is my plan: we must provoke a crisis, a serious one. The kind of crisis — for the sake of the security of the Most Holy Lodge and your own salvation — that would cause you to be sent far, far away. Elsewhere. And since all its branches have their roots in Sicily, that is where you'll go to disappear!"

"That sounds logical! And what will this grave crisis be?"

---

* Sacred Column–Sacred Council–Reign of the Heavens.

"We have to make it seem as if your life were in danger."

"But what's the crisis?"

"Me!"

"You? How's that?"

"I must die a sudden death . . ."

"You'll die?"

"Exactly. Immediately, people will rush to your aid and you'll be put in a safe place until everything blows over. You're a very precious human resource who's always done his work in exemplary fashion. And you know a lot, even if you know nothing. You'll be offered immediate protection. Logically, you'd be next on the list."

"Sudden death! That's not at all how I'd pictured things."

"Is that so? And how did you picture things? Did you ever picture them at all? No. You don't picture anything. You're in complete darkness, and I can lead you where you want to go. There, into the light . . . the light of Sicily!"

Silence.

"I am a *Maestro sicario* and a Very Honorable Member of the Most Holy Lodge. I know exactly who I am and where I am. I know what I like and I like what I know. I've thought long and hard about this and, believe me, there is only one solution. If you want to go to Sicily and search for your patriarchal olive tree, well, then, I'll have to be found murdered. Nothing more, nothing less."

"But I don't want to go that far!"

"You'll have to. You have a choice, but you don't have a choice: a false life or the patriarchal tree under the Sicilian sun. If I were you, at your age, in the incredible psychological imbroglio in which you find yourself, I wouldn't hesitate a single second. I'm old, I've lived my life, my false life. I would have given anything for a real one."

"But you'll die!"

"Not really, since I've never lived. I've spent my false life killing real ones. A fine irony for a *Maestro sicario!*"

"Dying doesn't bother you?"

"That's not the point."

The two men ate and talked slowly. The leg of lamb was good, but the sauce made of anchovies and rosemary overwhelmed the delicate taste of the meat. Besides, it made a man want to reach for the wine. And Olivo Oliva drank! The artichokes and fennel sprinkled with Parmesan were crunchy on the palate. Mr. Apandollo was enjoying the feast. The veal chops seasoned with the oil of Caltanissetta and Marsala caressed the tongue with each bite. It was good!

"Olivo Oliva, you know we'll have to act fast."

"I can't believe you're going to sacrifice your life for a sojourn in Sicily."

"You talk too much . . ."

"That's because you talked too much before me. Go

on, Mr. Apandollo, I'm sure you have more interesting ideas. I'm listening."

"Do you know how I'll have to die? Because there's only one way of doing things, just one."

"So we're back to that again? No, I don't know."

"Guess."

"Suicide, I suppose," Olivo Oliva said.

"Suicide! I could never do that. That's against the holy dispositions of the Very Holy Roman and Apostolic Catholic Church. I want a spot in a real cemetery, and I want paradise for all eternity. I've got hell on earth already. Go through it again? No thanks!"

"A car accident?"

"Then where's the grave crisis? Dying at the wheel of a car is a most regrettable circumstance, but no one will send you to Sicily for that. Think about it . . ."

"I don't get it . . . I really don't get it."

"We have to make it look as though an obscure and unknown group attacked and murdered me. That's where the crisis comes in: a war is beginning. For that to happen, I have to be discovered in an alley, the victim of a cruel and heartless murderer."

"That's so sordid!"

"Exactly. A sordid alley. So someone has to murder me. Naturally, I thought of you."

"Me?" Olivo Oliva cried.

"Stop shouting like that. There's no other solution. This involves both of us: you *and* me. Don't forget, we're plotting against something very high and very powerful: the Most Holy and Honorable Lodge. We have to act alone, you and I. Besides, who would dare suspect you?"

"But I can't go and kill you."

"Alas! And it can't be done just any way. What I mean is . . . you'll have to kill me, not like the artist you are — for that would be a signature — but like a common criminal, to throw them off the trail."

"This is crazy!"

"You are an olive in search of a patriarchal tree in Sicily. So which is crazier? You've convinced me: this is like a novel."

"The trip to Sicily was my project, and now it's become yours."

"Listen to me, Olivo Oliva. Every time you lift a finger, there are people who know which one you moved and when. So imagine a trip in an airplane, above the Atlantic Ocean, to Sicily! You said it yourself: I'm the only person on earth who can help you. You don't know how right you are! I've thought about it, I've analyzed the problem from every possible angle. There's no other way. I am extremely well placed, and the discovery of my corpse will cause consternation. And since you're my most faithful servant, you'll immediately be moved out of danger, to Sicily. From there, it's up to you . . . But that won't matter, I won't be there to advise you. I can picture my acolytes' faces when they learn of my death. It is a little funny . . ."

More silence.

"Do me a favor. Promise me you'll tread the earth of Sicily with both hands thrust deep in your pockets."

"Both hands deep in my pockets?"

"That's it."

"Okay. I promise to tread the earth of Sicily with both hands thrust deep in my pockets."

"Thank you."

Mr. Apandollo fell silent. He dipped his bread in the smooth sauce. He was proud, and pride, and the warm contentment it can bring, was a feeling whose existence he'd almost forgotten. He smiled.

Olivo Oliva was surprised by how carefully the *Maestro sicario* had thought out his plan. Every word had been weighed, every argument impeccably presented. No improvisation, and much circumspection.

"Mr. Apandollo, you're very persuasive, but you realize we've known each other for many years, and I have great affection for you. Yes, it's true. I wonder where I'm going to find the courage to . . ."

"And I have great affection for you, too. I wonder where I'm going to find the courage to let myself be slain by you."

"So?"

"So nothing. Be cynical, my friend, that's all there is to it. We will see each other again very soon, and that will be the last time. Invent a character for yourself and be cynical, be cynical, be cynical. For the love of God and the Most Holy Lodge *Sacro Colonnato–Santo Consiglio–Regno Dei Cieli*, be cynical."

"Mr. Apandollo, do you want me to kill you?"

"Olivo Oliva, do you want to find your olive tree in Sicily?"

"Mr. Apandollo, do you want it to be done in a cruel and sordid manner?"

"Olivo Oliva, do you want to sleep with the fishes?"

"Mr. Apandollo, aren't you afraid of death?"

"Olivo Oliva, aren't you afraid of life?"

"Mr. Apandollo, do you think this trip will be good for me?"

"Olivo Oliva, do you think that wine is good for me?"

"Mr. Apandollo, do you think your plan will work?"

"Olivo Oliva, do you think these jewels give off the scent of Sicily?"

"Mr. Apandollo, are you sure I'm going to land in Sicily?"

"Olivo Oliva, are you sure your olive tree is to be found in Sicily?"

"Mr. Apandollo, are you sure that the Most Holy Lodge is a Most Holy Lodge?"

"Olivo Oliva, are you sure that the Holy Roman and Apostolic Catholic Church is a Holy Roman and Apostolic Catholic Church?"

"Mr. Apandollo, will it hurt?"

"God, you ask questions!"

"Mr. Apandollo, will I be sad?"

"God, you ask them badly!"

A few days later, Olivo Oliva waited, slouching, in a doorway. He kept one shoulder propped against the wall. The alley was perfectly sordid and he promised himself that he'd be cynical, cynical, cynical . . . To pass the time, he watched the streams of clouds traveling across the sky, obscuring the moon that lit up the earth. In his right hand he held a sawed-off .12-gauge Beretta.

He knew Mr. Apandollo's habits. Tonight was opera night! And this alley was his favorite place for a walk after the show!

The *Maestro sicario* had also sworn to be cynical, cynical, cynical . . .

"Then what?" Poloni cried, his eyes alight.

"Then he showed up at the end of the alley."

"No! Are you sure?"

"He told me."

"He told you what?"

"That after the opera and the restaurant, he always walked home alone, down this alley."

"The whole thing's so unlikely! I never heard anything like it."

"Calm down, Poloni. I'll go get another bottle. In the meantime, take a few deep breaths and try to sit still for a minute."

A few minutes elapsed.

"Olivo Oliva, your nose is red again."

"As red as Marsala wine. My nose is always red after I've been in my Imaginary Museum. Because of the dust. I collect dust. You knew that, didn't you? Now, where's the corkscrew?"

"Here. Take it. Now, go on, go on."

"Where was I?"

"Mr. Apandollo showed up at the end of the alley."

"Oh, yes. I was in a doorway, and Mr. Apandollo came walking along — "

"And?"

"Stop interrupting me all the time, you're getting on my nerves! I'm losing my train of thought."

"Pardon me."

"So, Mr. Apandollo came walking along, nice and slow. When he passed me, I stepped out of my hiding place. I was wearing a mask."

"A mask?" Poloni repeated.

"Yes, it was a bit of whimsy on my part. I was wearing a Mickey Mouse mask."

"Mickey Mouse!"

"Yes, Mickey Mouse. And I had a sawed-off Beretta, too."

"A brand-new phantasmagorical animal. Absolutely beautiful! Just perfect! Did he recognize you?"

"Of course. Mr. Apandollo was wearing a mask as well."

"Him too?"

"Yes. He wasn't wearing one but two masks. One on his face and one on the back of his head. One tragic, the other comic. They were very old theatrical masks made of olive wood, with an opening for the mouth, like a megaphone."

"You mean those famous stylized Greek masks, with one face laughing and the other crying?"

"Exactly. He'd bought them from an antique dealer. They were very old, two thousand years old, maybe more. Mr. Apandollo always claimed that the history of world theater began in Sicily with Aeschylus. And since he was about to participate in a Sicilian tragedy, he wanted to experience it in the antique style."

"One plastic mask, and two wooden ones two thousand years old. Mickey Mouse versus Aeschylus! How emblematic can you get!"

"I hadn't thought about it that way. The idea was to be cynical, cynical, cynical. The only way, according to

Mr. Apandollo, to transcend and do what must be done."

"What dialectics!"

"You're right. Absolutely incredible . . . The most untoward experience of my false life! I stepped out of my hiding place with this Mickey Mouse mask on my face. Want more wine?"

"Yes, yes, please!"

"Calm down, all right? Look at your shirt, it's all wrinkled. Stop jiggling around, you're getting on my nerves. Now, where was I? Oh, yes! When he saw me, Mr. Apandollo cried out, 'Who goes there?' His voice echoed inside his wooden mask. The effect was terrifying, as if a chthonic rumble were issuing from the depths of the earth. It was dreadful! I answered, 'A cherub.'"

"But you were wearing a Mickey Mouse mask."

"Poloni, that doesn't matter!" Olivo Oliva shouted in exasperation. "It's not important since everything had to be cynical, cynical, cynical . . . Then he replied in a completely different tone, 'A cherub! Well, well. What kind of cherub? Plump and asexual like those in Baroque art?' My appearance seemed to amuse him."

"How did you answer?"

"I didn't."

"You didn't?"

"What kind of answer could there be?"

"I suppose you're right."

"Then Mr. Apandollo asked, 'What do you want from me, Mr. Cherub?' 'I want to kill you,' I replied. And it was true, I was there to kill him."

"Incredible! Then what did he say?"

"He started laughing. 'Interesting, very interesting . . . Why do you want to do that?' 'Because you're alive,' I told him."

"Ah!" Poloni sighed.

"'Is that reason enough?' he wanted to know. And I told him, 'It's one of the basic criteria.'"

"*Mamma mia*, what a quick mind!"

"You're absolutely right! Then he challenged me, 'What have I done to deserve such punishment?' And you know how I answered?"

"I couldn't begin to imagine."

"'Who spoke of punishment? Your heart is beating, too.'"

"'Your heart is beating, too.' That's so beautiful! Beautiful! I feel like crying. Quick, more wine! Then what happened?"

"Then I fired."

"You fired."

"Yes, I fired. With this."

Olivo Oliva passed the sawed-off Beretta to his friend.

"Two barrels of buckshot. His chest exploded. But Mr. Apandollo was still standing! Dead, and still standing! His back against the wall, his arms open like the wings of an airplane and his legs twisted. That kept him on his feet. The wooden masks didn't budge. They were perfectly adjusted, one comic, the other tragic. They seemed to fade into a delicate mist arising from his blasted chest and the cool of the evening. Something straight out of Dante! I left."

"Weren't you spooked? Weren't you sorry?"

"No. Weird, isn't it? Nothing at all! I was in a state. I didn't feel as if I'd slain Mr. Apandollo for the simple reason that, as I fired, I had the strange impression that the act had already been carried out, a long, long time ago. There was no reason to mourn since I had already mourned, in the past. Crazy! I felt as if I were on stage. A kind of nervousness. That's it, I was nervous! Imagine an actor who forgets his lines and realizes there's no one in the prompter's spot. I guess the masks heightened that feeling — that state of bewilderment."

The telephone rang.

"I'll be right back."

Olivo Oliva went to answer. The phone was at the far end of the studio. His friend Poloni picked up the Beretta lying on the glass table and examined it. The weapon was heavy and warm. Snug in the hand, with his index finger on the trigger, the gun communicated an urgent need to explode, an immediate desire for action.

Despite the modifications — which Olivo Oliva liked to call "successful cosmetic surgery" — the weapon, which had been manufactured, chiseled out and historicized by the most skillful craftsmen of the peninsula, retained its full measure of nobility and its legendary distinction.

The Beretta even shone with a sparkling new impropriety. Now here was a singular, unclassifiable weapon!

"Well, Poloni, things are falling into place."

"How's that?"

"The Most Holy Lodge just informed me of the death of Mr. Apandollo. I'm to be picked up in fifteen minutes and taken far away, out of all possible danger . . . to Sicily."

"Now that's Machiavellian! You're off to Sicily to complete your story. You really are an olive in search of a patriarchal tree!"

"Mr. Apandollo, may God grant his soul repose, saw things as they are. From this moment on, I'm part of something bigger. It's going to happen very quickly, so I must show you the door."

"I suppose so."

"Here, keep this as a souvenir."

"Your sawed-off Beretta!"

"Take it. It was used once, and its first time was its last. It won't be necessary where I'm going . . . Now, it's time to leave. Things are starting to take shape and none of this concerns you."

Olivo Oliva took his friend by the arm and escorted him to the door.

"I don't care for farewells. It's stupid to talk in those terms. This is the first time I've said goodbye to someone. It's odd. I think I might even feel sorrow. Our good friendship will be my best memory. You were the only person I could talk to. You helped me. You're a real person with a real life, a real erotic life filled with real women wrapped in a thousand ineffable perfumes. Women with real breasts, round and jovial, held tight in real cups, black, silky and taut. Breasts sensually decorated with nipples that swell when you murmur to them. Majestic breasts that point to the heavens like — "

"Like the dome of Saint Peter's in Rome!"

"Exactly!" cried Olivo Oliva.

"What's all that mean? I don't understand anything you're saying."

"Me neither . . . A flight of oratory from some unknown source. I am an actor, a painter, and I'm writing the chapters of a story. My life is a series of roles, canvases, mysterious sequences, and I've brought down many domes. I never had a real life. Everything happened in my thoughts . . . A constant sense that I'm about to touch soft, perfumed skin. An erotic delirium destroyed by the roughness of smashed stone. I know nothing of women, I know only their *morbidezza*."

"Why are you telling me this now, today?"

"Because I'm afraid. I'm treading water. Swimming in a sea of sadness. I know this trip won't change anything.

On the contrary — I sense that Sicily will magnify everything beyond all proportion. The landscapes will change, but my false life will remain false. I aspire to a real life with real, with real . . ." He paused. "Suddenly I feel so sleepy. I'm tired of talking . . . Mortally tired."

The two young men shook hands; their intensity was beautiful to see. The goodbyes dragged out. They promised postcards, endless letters and telephone calls. They swore they'd see each other soon, that their solid friendship would last forever. It was moving! But once the door closed, everything fell apart. As he went down the stairs to the street, Poloni knew he would never see his friend again. Alone in his studio, Olivo Oliva realized he'd just lost a brother. The two young men cried. One in the street, steadying a sawed-off Beretta under his coat, the other cursing his collection of dust.

A few minutes later, a "private," displaying flawless courtesy and superbly dressed in a suit a size or two too big, appeared at Olivo Oliva's door.

"Good day, Mr. Oliva. We spoke on the phone a few minutes ago. I'm sorry to hurry you this way, but I must drive you to the airport. Your plane for Palermo leaves in two hours. We barely have time to make it. I see that your suitcase is packed. I'll take it, if you like."

"I'll be right there. Go down without me, I won't be long."

"Please try and hurry, *signore*."

"I forgot one thing. I have to stop by the Russian shoemaker's shop. I had my favorite shoes resoled and I wouldn't leave them behind for anything in the world."

"Is it really necessary?"

"I'm afraid so."

"Mr. Oliva, I'll wait for you downstairs, with the car. Take this, it's for you."

The private handed him an envelope and disappeared down the stairs. It contained an airline ticket for Palermo, credit cards, a handsome pile of dollars, stacks of Italian *lira* and a passport. Olivo Oliva looked at the document and the photo, then read his new name: Toni Canari.

"Toni Canari! My name is Toni Canari! I am an olive in a sea of inertia. I am an olive in search of a patriarchal tree, an identity, a real life with real breasts . . . and my name is Toni Canari! One wing for Sicily, the other for America, and nothing in between to make them fly . . . except nostalgia, the obsession of a lifetime."

He grabbed a bottle of wine from the table and drank.

"My name is Toni Canari."

Olivo Oliva stepped into his Imaginary Museum. For the last time he contemplated his canvases, counted the fountain pens lined up in the display case, broke a ceramic dragon, splattered the zebra skin with blue paint, sneezed into the Norwegian flag and threw the bust of the Roman general against the photo of Mussolini with his fingers in his nose.

He took one last drink, then cast the empty bottle into the sea of dust. As a final farewell, he wrapped his arms around the *Greek Slave-Girl* with morbid affection, caressing her domes and applying lascivious kisses to her magnificent stone mouth that had never moved.

"A woman of stone, now, that's art," he murmured softly into the statue's ear.

The little bell in the shoemaker's shop tinkled; the bell was a tin can in which a bolt hung. It swung stupidly whenever the door opened or closed.

The Russian shoemaker wasn't Russian. He came from one of those Eastern Bloc countries where shoes are such a rare commodity, and their quality is so precarious and their function so ordinary that, apprentice without a master, he was wholly incapable of recognizing a well-made shoe, or doing good work, or being a good shoemaker. So why was he a shoemaker?

He threw the shoes on the counter. Olivo Oliva picked them up delicately as if they were two wounded fledglings fallen from the nest. In the hands of this brute, the shoes had been gravely mistreated. The leather was cut in a zigzag, the glue had squirted out from every crevasse and hardened, hairy sutures stuck out of the stitching, and the heels were misaligned. The young man didn't like the shoemaker. As he stepped out of his shop, he took particular care to memorize the carillon of that stupid chime.

It would be his last memory of North America.

III

*O*livo Oliva landed in Palermo with both hands thrust deep in his pockets, the fetid jewels in a third pocket and the massacred shoes on his feet. And now his name was Toni Canari! It was Toni Canari this, Toni Canari that . . .

Since that wild ride in an Alfa Romeo through the Sicilian countryside, Olivo Oliva had no idea where he was. And now he stood before a baroque palace built during the domination of Very Catholic Spain and ruined by centuries of neglect, telluric stress and the bombs of a young American pilot who smoked Lucky Strikes and chewed Wrigley's Spearmint.

The foundations oozed that same greenish snot and the roof beams stank of rancid oil. The rear wing, which was once a mountain of gravel and stone, had been smoothed out by the years. Now it was no more than a mound covered with slanting stakes where kidney beans grew. The plank lean-to housed guinea fowl and the pool still sheltered the kingdom of humble animals that slipped and slid and crawled and hopped and swam . . . And every laurel bush held captive a Bible, a crucifix and a set of tiny bones, still lily white.

Olivo Oliva was greeted by the two humpbacked sisters — the *sorelle cammelle* — and the two loitering, indolent men who wore out the shoulders of their shirts with the straps of their rifles. And by Signore Di Vita, the sovereign owner of this rundown domain adrift in a sea of olive trees.

This little universe hadn't moved since the death of Pina Di Vita and the birth of the little bastard. True, the residents had grown older, but not much.

No one suspected that the new guest who'd arrived from North America was that little bastard, in person: the son of Milli Palme and Pina Di Vita and, through allegory, the son of the wrinkled Olive that had promised to make war on the Patriarchal Tree. And, of course, the North American guest knew nothing of all that!

He was given the upstairs room, the vast oval salon, lapis-lazuli blue, overloaded with layers of ornamentation and inhabited by sweating mortadella. He slept in a canopy bed with sawed-off columns, the same bed Pina Di Vita had occupied during her pregnancy. The bed in which he was born. The bed where his mother died giving birth to him . . .

Under the sheets, the mattress was stained black. And Olivo Oliva took his rest on these dark stains!

One day, hoping to make a good impression, the North American guest made a move to shift the wheelbarrow full of broken plaster out of the way of the main door, whose normal movement it had been inhibiting for the last half century.

"Let me move the wheelbarrow, it's in the way . . ."

"Why are you doing that?" he was asked politely.

"The wheelbarrow is keeping the door from opening normally. Isn't it right to move it?"

"Opening normally! Just what are you talking about? Young man, life in North America might be a fast-moving thing. But here, in this obscure ruin adrift in a sea of olive trees, who's forcing you to do anything at all? Sicily is a triangular museum lost in the midst of the Mediterranean. And in a museum, you don't touch the exhibits!"

Olivo Oliva never touched anything again. He walked around, he stepped over, he jumped across, but never did he touch any of the centuries-old debris. If, by accident, he did move a stone, he immediately put it back in its proper place, for it was sacred, sacred insofar as it belonged to a museum lost in the Mediterranean.

Olivo Oliva understood the respectful consideration shown to hieratic objects. Hadn't he himself once been the possessor of an Imaginary Museum, and a collector of dust?

"In America, I used to collect dust."

"*Bravissimo!*" all around him exclaimed.

That morning, under the pergola covered over with vines and alive with huge, slimy, hairy spiders, Olivo Oliva, seated in front of an eggcup, was having his breakfast. In the sky, the swallows announced their departure for Africa. There were thousands of them. They twittered horribly, went wheeling in wide circles and spun in breathtaking disorder. Autumn, somewhere in Sicily.

The guest detested the sight. It had nothing in common with the order and majesty of Canada geese slipping across the sky towards the marshlands of the American Southeast. He didn't notice that a spider, as slimy and hairy as her sisters, had broken through her web and fallen into the eggcup. The poor beast drowned as a result of him dipping his bread in the yoke.

Olivo Oliva motioned to the two men loitering in the ruins. With his hands, he gave them a series of clear directives. There was no hesitation: the men let fly with blasts of birdshot at the countless swallows staining the sky. Fifty of them fell to the ground, dead. The others fled.

There! The sky was blue and the sun, climbing lazily towards noon, could carry on with its miserable task: driving human souls mad.

The young man motioned with his hand again. A single gesture. The two men smiled. That was their favorite game: shooting storms of lead at the sun.

"Cursed sun!" the two men called out.

"Cursed sun," Olivo Oliva said softly, finishing his breakfast.

He'd eaten everything. And he didn't feel very well. Nasty cramps twisted his belly, right there, and a funny taste flooded into his mouth. He went up to his room and stayed in bed five straight days, feverish, vomiting bile, his skin green.

"What's the matter with you?" the two humpbacked sisters asked, their voices gentle.

"I think the egg was alive."

"Poor little angel from On High . . ." they replied, their eyes wet with compassion.

Olivo Oliva was the idol of the household. He didn't talk much, and, best of all, he never asked questions. For once, a foreigner who didn't bother anyone.

In the evening, before sitting down to monstrous

cauldrons of *pastasciutta*, Olivo Oliva, egged on by the two men, performed his imitations of North American life. He aped the motions of baseball pitchers by throwing tomatoes; he chewed gum, Marlon Brando style; he moaned like a moose in heat; he sang "What a Wonderful World" in Louis Armstrong's gravelly voice; with bells on his feet, he mimed the rain dance of the Plains Indians; he strolled around as nonchalantly as Gary Cooper; and, most difficult of all, he smoked with the smugness of Humphrey Bogart. The two men laughed heartily. What entertainment! Finally, they were having some fun.

Besides, Olivo Oliva had taught them the new game: emptying your cartridge belt while cursing the sun.

The *sorelle cammelle* also appreciated the company of this polite, affable, famished young man.

"It does the heart good to see a young man eat so much, without even stopping to talk," said the first sister.

"And without asking a single question," said the second.

"For the best words are those we don't pronounce."

"And the best questions, the ones we keep to ourselves."

"It's a welcome change after those upper-class girls who come here knocked up and completely terrorized. God, how capricious they can be! And they hardly even touch their plates!"

"Ah, the she-devils! Now they go to Rome for their abortions. That cursed capital! Even today she's killing the sons of Sicily," the other sister declared.

Of all the inhabitants, Signore Di Vita was the most intrigued by the arrival of the new guest. Everything that came from North America had always fascinated him. His specialty was American mythology. After all, hadn't he organized the landing of several American and Canadian battalions on the island? Hadn't he been decorated by General Patton? With a band of cohorts, hadn't he plotted Sicily's sovereignty and her joining the United States of America as the forty-ninth state? Hadn't his failure left a bitter taste in his mouth? Hadn't he stolen the famous general's binoculars?

Often Signore Di Vita could be seen stepping down from his carriage at twilight, taking Olivo Oliva by the arm and leading him out to the large pergola full of slimy, hairy spiders. *Granita* was served, with almond biscuits, and the chairs were set in a line. That was the household's preferred pastime: they would gather around the North American guest, let ice melt in their mouths, drink cold white wine and strong coffee and ask, "Mr. Canari, tell us about North America."

"About North America?"

"They say that American automobiles are as big as locomotives. They say they can go as fast as rockets."

"Absolutely not, that's ridiculous," Olivo Oliva would answer.

"That's not true!" the household would retort.

"What do you mean it's not true? I lived all my life in North America. I've seen millions of automobiles. They're big, sure, but you can't compare them to locomotives. They're fast, that's a fact. But not as fast as rockets!"

"You just didn't look close enough," they answered unhappily.

Olivo Oliva presented things as they were, without exaggeration, without deforming reality. But these poor Sicilian ears would have none of it. Everything was bigger, grander, higher, stronger, faster and more beautiful in North America. Every detail took on hyperbolic dimensions that veered off into the burlesque. These people fell victim to their own mythology.

"Mr. Canari, tell us about North America!"

"Again?"

"Is it true there's a concrete stadium whose tower leans at the world's sharpest angle?"

"The tower exists. It's in Montreal. It's one hundred and seventy-five meters high at an angle of forty-five degrees."

"One hundred and seventy-five meters high at a forty-five-degree angle!" they exclaimed in wonderment.

"But the tower's a terrible mistake! An eccentricity that has no use! It costs a fortune in upkeep and it's so ugly no one wants to look at it. Oh, the tower exists all right, at a forty-five-degree angle — and it's perfectly grotesque. Now, the Tower of Pisa, that's a work of art!"

"The Tower of Pisa!" the *sorelle cammelle* whispered, making the sign of the cross.

"The Tower of Pisa!" the two men exclaimed, driven from their state of indolence as if a stiletto had been jabbed into their ribs.

"The Tower of Pisa!" Signore Di Vita cried, spitting out his ice.

"What? What did I say wrong?" Olivo Oliva asked.

Signore Di Vita didn't know what to think of the young man. His intuitive fear of life inspired mistrust. Every time he observed Olivo Oliva, he recalled the bastard that his late daughter had brought into the world, upstairs, in the oval room. And every time he pictured the child with his crown of flies, the words he'd pronounced thirty years earlier shattered the peace of his memory like an iceberg kept deep in the marine depths, bursting suddenly to the surface of a sea of oil.

He is as blue as the night, as green as the olive, and I fear him. At the height of his beauty and strength, when his testicles are as big as Lucca olives, he will return. They all return to the womb when vengeance calls them. In his veins flows the blood of his murdered parents. This little bastard will return to stand before me. I can feel fate speaking to me. It will fall upon me and my prosperity. I decapitated his father, repudiated his mother, crushed his identity and built the walls of his prison . . . The Sicilian who has suffered humiliation is as single-minded as the salmon in the month of May; one leaves the vastness of the Atlantic to spawn, the other the vastness of America to strike . . .

Sangu lava sangu . . . Sangu lava sangu . . . Sangu lava sangu . . .

"Mr. Canari, shall we get to know each other?"

"You are my host, Mr. Di Vita."

"Toni Canari, is that your name?"

"I was baptized Toni Canari before God. And no man can change that!" Olivo Oliva declared proudly.

"And what's your favorite color?"

"I like the blue of night, and I like the green of the olive."

"Tell me, Mr. Canari, do you like the salmon?"

"I don't like that fish. The salmon leaves the land for the sea, and the sea for the land."

"Do you know your origins?"

"A mix of blood and olive oil flows in my veins."

"Are you vindictive?"

"I have no family."

"What did you do in North America?"

"I was a *sicario*."

"The world's oldest profession!"

"The most noble, the most extravagant!"

"Is that all?"

"That's not bad as it is."

"Actually, it's quite a lot."

"And you know everything!"

"*Signore*, Toni Canari — that is your name?"

"Before God!"

"Mr. Canari, look at this stone. It hasn't moved for fifty years, since the house was accidentally bombed. This stone will remain right here, for centuries. I'm going to personally see to that. I'll make it my business. Now, that sounds easy. Yet it's a responsibility full of risks, just because it is so ridiculously easy. To keep this stone from moving over the next centuries is an immensely complicated mission, just because it is so simple . . . And if tomorrow the Most Holy Lodge asked me to take this stone and put it in my shoe, well, then, I'd have a stone in my shoe! You, Mr. Canari, when you stroll through the olive grove, do you not have a stone in your shoe?"

"You are my superior in the hierarchy, and I love you.

I will answer all your requests. Mr. Di Vita, I am Toni Canari and the stone I carry in my shoe hurts me. It has forever deformed the way I walk. I am unsteady. It will be my death, and this I know. I am the plenipotentiary of a difficult and sordid mission."

"The shoe can carry a stone . . ."

"I am a *sicario* and vengeance has called me to Sicily."

"And the shoe can displace stones . . ."

"To save Western art."

"To save Western art! Now that's a colossal, sacred mandate!"

"Absolutely insane!"

"I don't know much about art."

"Whereas I'm a specialist."

"Forgive my indiscretion, but it seems to me that's a lot of work for one man."

"It's much too much."

"To save Western art! It's like going off alone to conquer the sun."

"That's exactly what it is."

"I won't ask you anything more, for asking is talking too much. I admire your courage and abnegation before the Most Holy Lodge. Besides, you frighten me . . . It's all so fantastic. So absurd. I understand nothing of it. But tell me, Mr. *Sicario*, why Sicily?"

"Mr. Di Vita, I'm not sure of anything, but I believe

that Mediterranean thought, which became the Latin world, then the West, was born on this island."

"*Madonna!*"

"How right you are!"

"What are you going to do?"

"I am going to build a dome on this island. I am going to build a dome in Sicily."

"And where are the foundations to be sunk?"

"Who knows?"

"May God protect the dome . . . Do you know what the architecture will look like?"

"Mr. Di Vita, do you know how the Mediterranean became the Western world?"

"No."

"Neither do I! But I'm guessing that the trinity of the olive tree, the olive and olive oil has something to do with it. That's the architecture."

"Olive oil as one of the fine arts!" cried Signore Di Vita. "*Madonna Santa!* But where will all this lead you, young man?"

"I am a *sicario* who loves the Most Holy and Honorable Lodge *Sacro Colonnato–Santo Consiglio–Regno Dei Cieli*."

"That's too much for one man alone. Mr. Canari, if I may be permitted this one reflection, you are in an old country worn out by history. Everything takes a thousand times longer here than on the continent.

Whatever you do, don't be modern. By her nature, Sicily detests that which is new. Novelty disturbs her and prevents her from sleeping. And everything that disturbs sleep is suspect. Suspicion can act on the Sicilian like a sedative, assuaging all vehemence and annulling all will. But it can also push him into excess, and then, blades slip across skin with the gentle touch of pain and the sawed-off *lupara* blows apart rib cages. Mr. *Sicario*, I recommend that you not be modern."

"Then I'll be minimal."

"That's right. Be minimal, never modern." A silence fell. "Now, if you need anything . . ."

"I need time and stillness."

"Time and stillness are the two natural resources of Sicily." Another silence. "Mr. Canari, I am old and you are young. I don't like the young. Their youth accentuates my aging. And the more the young move, the older I become. They're insolent, in my opinion. Even their inaction is insolent. You're young, and full of action. Imagine how much I could detest you. The more I think about it, the more I do detest you. I am going now. Watch me, I am climbing into my carriage and I am returning home, to the village. I'm going home to sleep. I will make this one last request: this dome you are to build, this dome you are to bring down, will it disturb my sleep?"

"But you're not a work of art!"

"I know that. But I am an island on an island lost in the Mediterranean. I am an island on an island at the crossroads of the Orient, Africa and Europe."

"Oh!"

Olivo Oliva was an olive in search of a patriarchal tree. Every day, after lunch, he stood up and announced summarily, "I'm going for a walk." He wished the household, still at the table, a good day, then grabbed a bag and, displaying great care, stepped around the heaps of gravel, split beams, shards of marble, staved-in walls, blocks of stone, twisted ironwork and piles of stucco. He passed by the kidney beans and followed a stony path. Each time, he turned his head towards the sixteen balconies that ornamented the façade like so many loges in a stageless theater looking out on nothing. What decadence! The corbels, graced with scrolls, shells, leaves of the acanthus, pearls, foliage, pagan monsters wearing glasses and fantastic visages, were almost all dislocated, broken, fallen down, crushed, burst apart, laid to waste . . . The full-bellied ironwork, embellished with complicated, tumultuous figures, hung in strips, creating the grotesque effect of giant rags.

The path was bordered by acanthus. It led to the sea of olives.

The two men were relieved. The poor fellows had

been afraid they'd be asked to go on the expedition.

"To go out walking in that sea of olive trees when the sun's hot enough to split rocks . . . It's insane," the first man said.

"Like spending your vacation in a prison cell," the other man agreed.

"To go walking among the olive trees is something that's simply not done," the first humpbacked sister added.

"So why is he doing it?" the second sister wanted to know.

Olivo Oliva devoured olive trees. One by one, under the sun that burns your hair and opens crevasses in your skin. One by one, in the obsessive stridulation of the cicadas.

Every tree was alike in rows that stretched to infinity! They were all identical, all heavy with black fruit shimmering with green, and green fruit shimmering with black. The most dreadful monotony of all dreadful monotonies.

At times a scorpion or tarantula would capture the man's attention, but so rarely . . . At times he would pull a bottle of wine from his bag and drink.

The young man examined every tree. In three years, he had managed to inspect some one hundred thousand of them. Since the grove numbered more than three million trees, Olivo Oliva, after some quick calculations, concluded that he'd probably die here, drowned in a sea of olive trees!

But, one day, he heard the rhythms of this song, scarcely audible among the movements of nature and the imperial sun high in the sky:

Semu di terra, e a la terra a tutt'uri
La sorti nostra nni chiama e nni voli:
La terra assuppa li nostri suduri,
Vita uni duna e cunvorta lu cori.

The song was beautiful. It came from the distance, somewhere beyond a row of cypress trees. Further on was a centuries-old wall overgrown with wild vines and bougainvillea. There stood a little hillock where broom, almond, mastic and stunted fig trees grew. Then came a steep incline, just as rocky, and covered with hart's-tongue and flowering nopal. As he rushed down the slope, Olivo Oliva ran straight into a donkey. The animal stopped short. The poor beast was loaded down with a mountain of supplies, topped off by the two singing men: the Pizzi brothers! What a small world!

"Now look at that, a wet shirt," the first brother declared.

"That sure is one wet shirt," the second brother chimed in.

"And the hair . . . the face . . . Yet there's no spring or water trough anywhere around here. Not even a damp hole in the ground. So it must be sweat."

"With a sun like this! But when you look closer, you see that the shirt is actually oily."

"It's completely oily, that shirt! And the hair! The face! If I didn't know better I'd say, here in the sun's heat, that the fellow was secreting an oily substance."

"Among the olive trees, anything is possible. Let's get a closer look at this phenomenon never before recorded in the annals of olive-growing."

"Indeed, we will. Let's have a look at this olive that stands on two legs and smells of oil."

The two brothers climbed down from their perch and stepped up to the man.

"I am Carlo Pizzi and this is Dario Pizzi. We are the Pizzi brothers. The greatest olive-cultivators in Sicily, in all the Mediterranean. Even if none of these trees belong to us. Even if this land we love isn't ours. We're still the greatest!"

"We are the greatest, though we don't possess as much as an olive pit. Imagine that! But we have this donkey. His name is Tito Asino and the tax department is after his ass. Poor animal! Such misery pursues him!

And you, young man, what are you doing in this sea of olive trees?"

"I'm taking a walk."

"You're taking a walk!" the two brothers cried.

The animal was drowning in its own slaver.

"Look, you've frightened our donkey. You frightened him with this story of taking a walk. You don't take a walk in an olive grove! It's like taking a walk in hell. Young man, I don't know how old you are, and I don't know how long you've been practicing this bad habit, but I can read faces, and you have aged twenty years in one day!"

"My brother is right. A person doesn't go walking among the olive trees. It's just not done! Look at yourself. Your back is bent from passing under the leaves that are too low, your hands are callused from touching short, sharp branches, you're walking sideways because of the slippery stones. The sun has made your hair fall out, it's burnt your skin, and your face is like an old parchment. What's more, the olive tree has a very bad effect on the spirit, it can bring on nightmares, even when you're awake."

"Nightmares, even when you're awake," the other brother echoed.

"You walk and you suffer! You do both, then you lie!"

"Inevitably, Mr. . . . Mr. what?"

"I am Toni Canari, and I'm from North America."

"Young man, Toni Canari is a name you give a bird, a canary, not a human being. The way Tito Asino is a name befitting a donkey, but not a man," one of the brothers pointed out.

"Your accent isn't from around here, I can tell that much. Besides, in North America, they cook with butter. So why are you here, among these trees that drive you to such suffering?" asked the other brother.

"I am the guest of Signore Di Vita," Olivo Oliva replied.

"We know Signore Di Vita, and we know him well! We've known him for decades. Signore Di Vita never invites anyone into his home. Especially not a North American who's crossed the Atlantic to go walking in a sea of olive trees at the hour when the vipers come out."

"Mr. Bird . . ."

"Canari. Toni Canari."

"Pardon me! Mr. Canari, my brother and I have a little job to do, up there, on that promontory that juts out. Nothing complicated, but it has to be done. Then we're going to eat and get some rest. Why don't you come with us? We can talk over this problem in a calm tone of voice. It would be an honor for us."

"It's true, and a pleasure, too. You must be tired, what with all your walking and all your lies."

"I'll come with you," Olivo Oliva decided.

The Pizzi brothers climbed back on the donkey. They were satisfied. They'd gotten the best of a North American. They smiled. The animal labored on. One last section of steep slope remained. The poor donkey, blinded by the hundreds of flies and wasps attracted to his slaver, staggered forward, its hooves seeking purchase between the big rocks with each stride. Olivo Oliva followed in silence.

The Pizzi brothers had spoken the truth. Olivo Oliva had changed. The young man suddenly realized it. He had lost the natural elegance that once distinguished him: his city ways, his broad shoulders, his animal litheness, his lively features, his well-combed hair, his sparkling eyes and haughty air — all that had disappeared.

His face was burned, shiny and crisscrossed with tortuous violet veinlets. He had acquired a third generation of puffy bags under his eyes. His teeth were rotting. His breath stank of gamy meat. His hair fell out with every stroke of the comb. His walk was beginning to resemble the swinging gait of an ape. His back had taken on a permanent curve that no orthopedic treatment could correct. And the ring of fat that had blossomed around his waist was no lifebelt!

Walking aimlessly among the olive trees under a hellish sun, tucking into giant plates of pasta swimming in oil, drinking liters of wine at every meal — in three years, the slim, energetic young man had turned into a prematurely aged and neglected creature.

Olivo Oliva gazed upon himself. He followed in the donkey's footsteps and murmured, "God, I'm ugly . . . I'm so ugly . . . So ugly . . ."

When they reached the top, they had to struggle miserably to remove the pack, it was so heavy. The poor little donkey was covered with a paste of insects mixed with slaver and blackish blood. While one brother washed down the animal and rubbed its nostrils and tongue with anisette, the other brother laid down a blanket near a cluster of broom flower, opened a parasol and motioned Olivo Oliva closer.

"Mr. Sparrow . . ."

"No. Canari. Toni Canari."

"Mr. Canari, my brother and I have some work to do. Duty calls. It'll take an hour, no more. In the meantime, lie down here in the shade. Watch us work. You've never seen olive-cultivators work, I'm willing to wager. Well, you're in for a surprise. Pardon me if I laugh, but it's really too funny. You want something to drink? We have white wine and red wine in the ice chest."

"White."

"Very good, I'll be right back. Don't move, make yourself at home."

The cicadas fell silent and the sea breeze was balm for Olivo Oliva after the torture of the sun. From the summit, lying in the shade of the parasol, he had a panoramic, fabulous view of the empty sea of olive trees. It was an impressive sight. The grove stretching on forever was frightening. As mysterious and harrowing as the Amazon forest must have been for the first Spanish explorers.

"The conquistadores," he thought, "went walking through the hell of the Amazon. They suffered from gold fever, and were swallowed up by the forest. And they murdered . . . What about me? For three years I've been looking for an olive tree to help write my story. What madness!"

For the first time, Olivo Oliva realized that taking a walk in the olive grove was something that simply wasn't done. And combing them in search of a patriarchal tree suddenly seemed like a terrible aberration.

"Mr. Finch!"

"Canari."

"Mr. Canari, you shouldn't stare at the olive trees that way. You will lose your power to reason. Losing your reason in a sea of this kind, you can imagine . . ."

The Pizzi brothers set the ice chest in the shade. It looked heavy, with its dozen bottles covered in chipped ice.

"Mr. Pizzi, may I ask you a question?"

"Why not?"

"You're an olive-cultivator?"

"The best."

"What does an olive-cultivator do?"

"What kind of question is that? I am an olive crafts-man. I care for trees. I understand them."

"You understand trees?"

"My dear young man, the olive tree has a psychology. I'm a psychologist, you understand?"

"Not really."

"Well, watch us work and you'll understand. Red wine or white?"

"White."

"Here you are."

"Thank you."

"I'm putting the bottle back in the ice, but don't be shy."

"You're an olive-cultivator and you have work to do. But I don't see a single tree on these heights."

"Not a single tree? On the contrary, the most presti-gious one is here! Before your eyes you have a very old olive tree."

"Where?"

"Right there, in front of you."

"That shattered, twisted pole?"

"That shattered, twisted pole is the oldest olive tree in the Mediterranean. It yielded its first fruit when Sicily was still under Arab occupation."

"Which was when?"

"The Arabs first set foot here in the ninth century."

"So the tree is more than a thousand years old!"

"It's the oldest olive tree in the Mediterranean. In this part of the world, we call it the Patriarchal Tree."

"The Patriarchal Tree!" Olivo Oliva exclaimed.

"Yes, the Patriarchal Tree. Every tree before you, as far as your eyes can see, descended from this one. Through grafts and layering. You seem extraordinarily interested, and your glass is empty already. The bottle is right there."

"That crooked thing is the oldest olive tree in the Mediterranean?"

"You're so excited all of a sudden! Yes, it's the oldest one. The sire of this sea that disturbs the senses."

"That's magnificent! Can I come and look? Can I touch it?"

"No!" A short silence fell. "This is no whim on our part. You cannot touch the Patriarchal Tree for the simple reason that the tree is dead."

"The Patriarchal Tree is dead!"

"Dead for thirty years. And one must not touch dead things. But we're olive-cultivators, and we have the right to do as we wish. But who are you? You don't touch dead things, it's not done."

"But the tree looks like it's alive. The branches are all there. The leaves are green. I can even see some fruit — "

"Wait here, I'll be right back."

One brother went to speak with the other. They talked and laughed together. Then they began sorting through the boxes and under the tarpaulins. There was a complete set of garden tools, a battery of kitchenware and long cardboard boxes with Chinese lettering on the side.

Inert and stupefied, the donkey seemed to be following the proceedings.

"I'm coming!" the Pizzi brother called, displaying one of the long boxes victoriously.

A broad smile split his face.

"Look at this, Mr. Nightingale."

"Canari. My name is Toni Canari."

"Sorry, Mr. Canari. Inside this box is the secret of our art."

"What is it?"

"Open it."

"Branches?"

"Olive branches."

"Olive branches?"

"Olive branches with real green and black olives on them."

"I don't get it."

"You don't get it? But what could be more simple! The Patriarchal Tree is dead. But we want it to live. So we built a little set."

"A set?" Olivo Oliva asked.

"Yes. A theatrical creation. Every year, for the last thirty years, at the same time, we scale this promontory, we eat, we drink wine and, most importantly, we freshen up the Patriarchal Tree. A little like an embalmer freshens up a corpse to make it look alive. Except we do a better job! For are we not the Pizzi brothers, the best olive-cultivators in the Mediterranean? A little patina, a little paint to bring out all the shades of the bark. Varnish to restore its former brilliance. Look! This comes from China! Fake olive branches made from a mixture of natural silk and synthetic resin. Admire the leaves, you'd swear they were real. I'm an olive-cultivator, and I can't tell the difference. And these olives! Examine them. All hand-painted! What a finish! What art! The problem is that cursed sun. The colors have a tendency to fade . . ."

"So you come here every year to repaint the tree and change the leaves and the fruit bleached by the sun?"

"You have a simplistic way of putting things, but that's about it."

"And Signore Di Vita doesn't suspect anything?"

"For all these years, he's been completely satisfied with our work, and for all these years, we've been well paid . . . Signore Di Vita is a very touchy man, and very pessimistic, too. That's why he's invested so much money and made such an effort to keep his tree alive. And the tree *is* alive! Alive according to our definition, of course, but alive all the same . . . Now, whether or not the Patriarchal Tree is alive according to Signore Di Vita's definition, who could say?" A brief silence. "In any case, we had no choice. The tree had been sentenced to die."

"Sentenced?"

"It's a rather somber story. Some thirty years ago, a very bold young man wanted to kill the Patriarchal Tree and cause the downfall of the Di Vita family. A family who had reduced his own to poverty."

"What courage!"

"Very heroic indeed. The young man almost succeeded, but Signore Di Vita realized what was happening, and he sent for us immediately. We are the best, and we saved the Tree."

"Then how come the tree is dead if you saved it?"

"It was murdered."

"Who did it?"

"The other olive trees."

"The other olive trees murdered the Patriarchal Tree?"

"Just as I said. A kind of parricide of the plant world."

"Why did they do it?"

"Who knows? That's the way it is. Despite everything we did, the Patriarchal Tree never truly recovered from the injuries inflicted by the young man. The tree was alive, it sent out new leaves, it produced some fruit, but it had become . . . senile, you might say."

"And then?"

"I'm not so sure. The other trees sentenced it to death. And they murdered it."

"How?"

"Vegetable magnetism."

"How can you claim that an olive tree is senile?"

"You have to be an olive-cultivator to know for sure. My brother and I feel these things instinctively. That's why we're the best. Not only are we botanists, we can read the soul of the tree. It might sound funny, but that's the way it is. The olive tree is not just a piece of vegetation that lives off water, earth and light. It's amazing how much deleterious energy this tree can emit. And you have to be Sicilian to be an olive-cultivator! We Sicilians have this pathological obsession with silence. We have pushed silence to a cacophonous height! For us, a taciturn man is an incorrigible babbler, and the quietude of a hamlet sounds like a noisy village feast. I read the silence and inertia of an olive tree, while you read the newspaper. You seem perplexed, yet . . . I read the death of the Patriarchal Tree the way you read an obituary." Another brief silence. "Sorry, I have to work. The ice chest is there. My brother and I will be right back."

"What happened to the young man who wanted to kill the Patriarchal Olive Tree?"

"He went to America."

"North America?" Olivo Oliva wanted to know.

"No. Mythological America. Where is he? Who knows? He's dead . . . He's alive . . . He's alive and he's dead . . . One thing's certain, wherever he is, he's in a mythological territory. The young man wanted to kill the Great Patriarchal Olive Tree of the Mediterranean, a sponge that's been dripping myth and legend ever since Antiquity. What would you expect? — the kid got splattered in the process. Where is he? Who knows? He's somewhere in America the way Ulysses is somewhere on a stormy sea."

"Can I ask you another question?"

"Why not? You ask them so badly."

"Are you sure the Patriarchal Tree is dead?"

"I myself witnessed this plant parricide. I watched the tree's death throes. I watched it die thirty years ago. It might look alive, but that's just proof that the Pizzi brothers are the best olive-cultivators in Sicily. We order our colors and varnishes from Holland, and the branches heavy with leaves and fruit come to us from China. The Patriarchal Tree is dead. God rest its soul . . ."

"One last thing: why are you telling me all this? You and your brother have been swindling Signore Di Vita for all these years, and now you give away the whole story, right down to the tiniest detail, as if you trusted me. That's completely anti-Sicilian!"

"Mr. Warbler . . ."

"Canari."

"Mr. Canari, there are two categories of people who go walking among the olive trees — and considering your appearance and the way you keep rearranging reality, we can see that's your only activity. Two categories: people living clandestinely for extraordinary reasons, and crazies! Whether you're one or the other, or both, we appreciate that. And, God, do you ever stink of olive oil! We appreciate that, too. Very much." A quick silence. "Excuse me, I really do have to go to work."

Olivo Oliva watched the Pizzi brothers. Carlo, with a palette of subtle shades and natural varnishes, was retouching the Tree's bark. Dario was delicately pulling off the ruined branches and replacing them with new ones whose colors were definitely more lifelike. Watching these craftsmen was a pleasure. They were possessed with the attitude and awareness of another age. They worked slowly because working fast serves no purpose. They didn't talk because you don't talk when you work. They were antiques — therein lay their wealth!

Olivo Oliva was moved.

An hour later, the Pizzi brothers were circling the tree slowly and adding the finishing touches: a little black here, red there, more varnish at the very bottom. This branch was too high, the other too low, and these too long . . .

The Patriarchal Tree was a new Patriarchal Tree. It appeared to be in full possession of its youth. At the top of the promontory, the tree shone with absolute authority as the sole sire of the grove and oldest tree in the Mediterranean. It was sovereign and cruel, like its friend, the sun. The dead Olive Tree looked alive, so everyone was happy.

The Pizzi brothers were happy because they had done good work. Craftsmen are often filled with sweet felicity after a job well done. They can be so sensitive . . .

And Olivo Oliva, realizing that the Patriarchal Tree was no more than a varnished post topped with plastic branches and leaves, was just as happy.

"Cursed literature . . . Cursed literature . . . Cursed literature," he muttered as he slurped down the wine, wearing his best smile.

"After a job well done, we eat!" the olive-cultivating brothers announced happily.

They opened a second parasol, unfolded a table and chairs, spread out the tablecloth, set out the utensils and plates, uncorked the bottles, boiled the water, fried the eggplant, sautéed the scallopini and heated the sauce. The bread was good, the melons well cut, the ham sliced perfectly, the Parmesan ready to grate, the olives well grilled and the red peppers completely drowned.

The meal was taken in high spirits. After the *antipasti*, they demolished a scandalously large cauldron of *pasta-*

sciutta, kilos of scallopini, and a dozen bottles were emptied. They talked about everything . . . Absolutely everything . . . Sicily and her history, the first olive trees brought to the island by Phoenician sailors, the Patriarchal Tree and the olive grove, Signore Di Vita and his skulduggery, the young man who'd wanted to kill the Tree by slashing love poems into its trunk. The Pizzi brothers even tried to recite a few verses, but unsuccessfully. They had forgotten everything. And of course, they spoke of America!

"Mr. Hummingbird . . ."

"Canari."

"Pardon me. Mr. Canari, is it true that in North America the automobiles are as long as rockets and fast as locomotives?"

"Not that again! No, the cars are normally long and go normally fast."

"That's not true," the Pizzi brothers said, crestfallen.

After the meal, they packed up their materials and loaded them onto the donkey. Poor little animal!

"Mr. Nuthatch . . ."

"Canari."

"Yes, of course, Canari. Listen carefully. My brother and I are going to get on the road now. It would be preferable if you stayed here at least another hour before leaving. You see, Signore Di Vita spends all day inspecting his trees, and it would not be prudent if all

four of us were seen together. When I say all four, I'm
including the donkey, of course. Signore DiVita is a very
suspicious man. And we possess a terrible secret!"

"My brother is right. Let us be prudent and we will
live long lives. Do you see those cypress trees over
there? Behind them is a little road. You live in that villa
that looks like a giant meringue, right?"

"A giant meringue? Yes, if you like . . ."

"Take the road to the left and you'll be there in
two hours. And do me a favor: stop walking among
the olive trees. You're walking in hell and you don't even
know it."

"Indeed! You're doing something that just isn't done.
Here, take this bottle, it's the last one and the best. Have
a seat in the shade and wait out the hour."

"Next year, same month, the day after the full moon,
my brother and I will have this same little job to do . . .
And you, young man, where will you be? Who knows?
If you're still on the island, consider yourself invited.
Come and spend the afternoon with us. And when I say
'us,' I include the donkey, of course."

"We'll meet here, in a year, at the foot of this corpse.
There will be plenty to eat and plenty of wine to drink."

"There will be colors and varnishes from Holland . . ."

"And branches and olives from China," Olivo Oliva
added, joining the game.

"So now we are accomplices," one brother said.

"Bravo! You understood. Now you're one of us. And when I say 'us,' I exclude Tito Asino for, you see, a donkey is a donkey is a donkey before God," the other brother concluded.

They shook hands in the most cordial manner possible. The farewells were sincere and interminable.

The Pizzi brothers climbed atop their mountain of supplies, and the animal began stumbling down the steep slope. Their hands, as they waved goodbye, flew like the sails of a windmill.

They began to sing:

Semu di terra, e a la terra a tutt'uri
La sorti nostra nni chiama e nni voli:
La terra assuppa li nostri suduri,
Vita uni duna e cunvorta lu cori.

Olivo Oliva returned to his spot by the broom flower. He rummaged through his bag and found the box, opened it and examined all that gold that played with the sun. He slipped the long chain around his neck; the *Trinacria* came to rest on his chest. Over his heart.

"Since this smell belongs to me," he said out loud.

Then he picked up the bracelet, ripped the charms off it one by one and threw them over the edge of the cliff. Every last one. The Doric column. The stiletto. The hand. The eye. The sun. The spear-shaped leaf. The olive and the olive tree. Every last one, except the replica of Sicily with its inset diamond. He closed the bracelet around his wrist and threw the box away.

"What a relief," he thought. "Frankly, this whole story was becoming intolerable. What a brilliant humiliation! The sire of the Mediterranean . . . The Most Royal Patriarchal Tree. The witness to every one of Sicily's invaders, the tree that imposed its millenary authority on all the other trees of the Mediterranean, killed by its own scions . . . What baseness! What perfidy! And tarted up for the last thirty years like a Sicilian puppet on Saint Agatha's Day! Could there be anything more pathetic?"

Olivo Oliva rummaged through his sack again. He was looking for the novel he was reading, *Treasure Island*, by Robert Louis Stevenson. He opened it at page 118 and began to read out loud. There was nothing else to do, and he needed to kill the seconds . . .

Another time he came and was silent for a while. Then he put his head on one side, and looked at me.

"Is this Ben Gunn a man?" he asked.

"I do not know, sir," said I. "I am not very sure whether he's sane."

"If there's any doubt about the matter, he is," returned the doctor. "A man who has been three years biting his nails on a desert island, Jim, can't expect to appear as sane as you or me. It doesn't lie in human nature. Was it cheese you said he had a fancy for?"

"Yes, sir, cheese," I answered.

"Well, Jim," says he, "just see the good that comes of being dainty in your food. You've seen my snuff-box, haven't you? And you never saw me take snuff, the reason being that in my snuff-box I carry a piece of Parmesan cheese — a cheese made in Italy, very nutritious. Well, that's for Ben Gunn!"

Olivo Oliva lifted his head. He took out his weapon. A black pistol whose serial number had been filed off. He smiled, aimed and fired. A bullet . . . Just one . . . Right there! In the center. Right in the heart . . . Cursed sun!

"What's the difference between a dead Patriarchal Tree made up with plastic leaves and fruit, and a lemon in place of a canary?" he asked out loud.

He was proud. The riddle was complicated, the way he liked them.

Then he went back to his reading.

Sicily, with her inset diamond, moved every time the young man turned a page or took a sip of wine.

Meanwhile, all the underskirts of Sicily were black . . . A blackness so penetrating it stupefies the eye and casts it into the most delectable excess.